DAVI

Lady Thatcher's Wink

POMEGRANATE PRESS

*Author's note: any resemblances between
the fictional characters in this book and
figures in British public life are intentional*

Published by Pomegranate Press, Lewes, Sussex
pomegranatepress@aol.com
www.pomegranate-press.co.uk

ISBN: 978-1-907242-60-1

This novel is also available as an e-book
ISBN: 978-1-907242-61-8

Cover design by David Marl
www.davidmarl.co.uk

Other Pomegranate Press fiction by the same author:
Cultic Cyphers from Celtic Cyprus (7,5) – Mr Douglas O'Dale's
  unique guide to solving cryptic crossword puzzles
Maracas in Caracas – short stories from England and the Americas

British Library Cataloguing-in-Publication Data
A catalogue record for this book is available from the British Library

Printed and bound by 4Edge, 7A Eldon Way, Hockley, Essex SS5 4AD

For Jill

WHO'S WHO in the novel

ANTHROPOLOGY TWO A young woman graduate with unquenchable artistic leanings.

APPLIED MATHEMATICS Martin, a graduate with a chronically poor sense of balance.

FRANK BLUDGEON Chief feature writer for the *Daily Maul*.

JASON BLURT Trenchant current affairs presenter for BBC radio.

JUSTIN BODGERS The government's Neutrality Overseer, Broadcasting, *aka* NOB.

TERRY BOLT Head of news for the BBC.

LORD BOTTING OF BOTTING Armaments dealer and Tory donor.

GLORIA BRIGHTBLOOM Chief communications adviser for the Labour Party.

JOHN CARROT Rebarbative taxi driver with an unfortunate Arsenal FC obsession.

CHARLES III King.

DEEPAK CHAUDHRI Carpet importer and reluctant father of Taz.

DAPHNE Power4Us Cleaning Operatives Organiser Grade 2, food bank volunteer and general good egg.

PC DUNNOCK A hapless police officer carefully coached in evil.

CHARLIE FLOUT Benefits claimant with multiple disabilities, not least Gregg Gripp.

LUKE FREEMANTLE Sports editor for the *Maul*.

DALTON FRISBY *Daily Maul* editor and would-be power in the land.

FREEMAN GOODBLOW Former disgraced prime minister blithely unashamed of his past.

FRED GORMSTHWAITE Men Fight Back party candidate.

GREGG GRIPP Rhadamanthine Power4Us handouts assessor.
JONATHAN The prime minister's loyal PPS.
FITZROY JULIAN Downing Street's chief of staff.
STRETTON MATHERS An extravagant artist.
SIR HILARY MILES-TRUMPINGTON Tory grandee and trustee of the Royal Academy.
MONTY MUCKLE Roguish leader of the nationalistic Excalibur Party.
VALMAI PARTRIDGE Pneumatic leader of the Pink Party.
PIMPKIN The king's sheepish private secretary.
LAMBERT PROBUS A ruthless chancellor of the exchequer.
MR ROSEJOY aka CURVATURE Handouts claimant with a vengeful streak.
HARRY SCUTT News editor at the *Maul*.
ARNOLD SNITCH The *Maul*'s chief leader writer.
CHLOE SOMERVILLE Our impossibly desirable heroine.
ALAN SPROUT Stodgy leader of the Labour Party.
ELLIE STAMMERS Gripp's adoring assistant.
BEN STRUTTERS A vicious, rapidly promoted, police officer.
TAZ An infamous blogger.
MRS THREADGOLD A risibly gullible frequenter of her local food bank.
TITCH TUPPER The smallest photographer on Fleet Street.
GERRY TURTLE The prime minister's chief press secretary and the epitome of oiliness.
DIANA WARBYTTON The prime minister's excitable daughter.
FREDDIE WARBYTTON The prime minister's scapegrace son.
JESSICA WARBYTTON The prime minister's semi-detached wife.
STURGEON WARBYTTON Caretaker Tory prime minister turned rabid revolutionary.
FERGIE WOOD Art director at the *Maul*.
YOUSSEF A tatooist.

"No society can surely be flourishing and happy, of which the far greater part of the members are poor and miserable."
– *Adam Smith*

"There is no such thing as society."
– *former premier Margaret Thatcher*

"Political language . . . is designed to make lies sound truthful and murder respectable, and to give an appearance of solidity to pure wind."
– *George Orwell*

"A week is a long time in politics."
– *former premier Harold Wilson*

FRIDAY

His death confidently pencilled in for six days hence, Sturgeon Lafayette Eggerton Warbytton was feeling rather less grand than his name demanded.

'Cheer up,' sang his odiously irrepressible companion. 'All to play for.'

'On a distinctly sticky wicket.'

'With the bails still on, Stu.'

'But the light fading fast.'

It was a futile analogy, but if Turtle insisted on carrying on with it he'd transport them both to a match he'd contested during an amateur tour of the West Indies many years ago – what they used to call darkies (Turtle had managed to train him out of that) hurling vicious balls down a grassless runway in the murk with the last pair in, he with his guts dissolved by a stew of unrecognisable native rodents and, he assumed, their nesting material, recklessly consumed the night before, his companion hobbled by the bite of a pit viper disturbed in its tussocky lair while fielding at long-on, with fifty needed to win. And no, they didn't bloody play up and play the game, but a bouncer had taken out his two front teeth and, churning blood, he'd fallen back on the stumps with a less than heroic gurgle. That's what it felt like now, should anyone care to ask.

'Only four of the little shits still to see. Or maybe it's five.'

That the death foretold was constitutional in the political rather than physical sense offered not a tincture of consolation. What was the difference? Six generations of Warbytton male babies had sucked in essence of Westminster from their complaisant mothers' dugs, had flexed their maturing muscles in hideously expensive, supposedly character forming, schools before, come the onset of their young flowering manhood, striding into the safest Tory seats in the shires. They were an

Lady Thatcher's Wink

undemonstrative bunch, rarely troubling Hansard, but not a single one of them had ever let the side down, unless you counted great uncle Cuthbert's incident with the parlour maid and the Gibraltar ape, and that never got beyond the village tongues and a gossip columnist who was bought off with a trunk of cash and an off-the-record visit from the maid. He was about to become the first.

'And who's this particular shit?' he asked.

It was too late to avoid immersion in his tormentor's view of the world, let alone his ripe language. The scheming Turtle was responsible for everything that had happened to him since the dreadful day, six months ago, that he was untimely ripped from standing shoulder to indifferent shoulder with his forefathers in blessed obscurity. Now (he gazed down from the second-floor window to the pitiless, cordoned-off emptiness of Downing Street) he was no less than First Lord of the Treasury and Prime Minister of the United Kingdom of Great Britain and Northern Ireland. Newspapers routinely lower-cased the job titles these days, but they were punishing capitals for Warbytton. It was unbearable.

'The taxi man. You know the rules. Sound sympathetic, but don't promise anything. *Semblance*, remember.'

'We won't have anything to give.'

'Indulge me, Stu. Trust me. We're going to pull this off.'

And who could doubt Gerry Turtle? It was impossible to imagine any nimble fingers but his – long, sinuous, indecently expressive now as they skipped reassuringly along his pupil's shoulder, concluding with a gentle farewell tap – capable of plucking up the jagged shards of a shattered party and reassembling them with such deftness that, as long as you didn't approach too closely, the abused artefact looked much the same as before . Of course the glued cracks were showing, in the way of today's fastidious museum repairs, but the

Friday

supreme trick was to have the precious relic carried into the light of day by a stolid, four-square caretaker who couldn't for a moment be thought to have caused the accident in the first place and clearly wasn't going to drop the thing all over again.

As Turtle left by one door, an all-knowing young PPS knocked on another, stepped inside and, wordlessly, raised his eyebrows high over a pair of steel-rimmed glasses. He stood back to usher in a paunchy middle-aged man with chest hairs sprouting above a tie-less check shirt. His black trousers were heavily creased and a little stained, and he wore red and white trainers stamped with the Arsenal Football Club logo.

'Mind if I sit down?' he asked after a token handshake. 'Not used to standing about.'

The hand Warbytton had briefly taken was not, as he had expected, flour white, plump, hairless and perhaps giving off a polished glow from its morning's labours: it was distinctly grubby, the fingers sprouted dark tangles of vegetation and the nails were bitten.

'I do believe you'd enjoy our splendid array of trophies on the wall at Eggerton Manor,' he began by way of an ice-breaker. 'Mr . . .'

'You what?' came the uncompromising reply.

His prejudice had led him to expect a calm, contemplative character. This alone should have alerted him to his mistake, but there had been so many improbabilities these last few weeks, so many semi-deranged people to see, that his guard was down. Had he consulted the visitors' book, he would have realised that his appointment with Taxidermists Preserving Britain was scheduled for midday tomorrow. This high noon, as he should have known, it was the turn of the capital's chippy taxi drivers.

'Stags mainly. Oh, I never hunted much myself,' he added quickly, remembering Turtle's no-controversy rule. 'Mr . . .'

'I'm John Carrot.'

'Not that I suppose you run across many Monarchs of the Glen these days.'

'In a word, guvnor, no. I'm not sure the insurance would cover it.'

'Let alone Bengal tigers, I'd wager.'

Carrot inclined his head expressively.

'You'd be right.'

'But still some foxes?'

'Road kill champions.'

'Surely not!'

'You can't avoid 'em. A lot of flattened dogs and cats, too.'

Warbytton, not an imaginative man, found himself at a loss to envisage the delicate labour required.

'The owners must be *very* appreciative of what you do.'

There fell a silence which in truth felt a tad menacing.

'I mean, making such an effort to reconstruct their pets' beloved features,' he faltered. 'Perhaps the little tail sometimes left defiantly up in the air, as if in the act of wagging – a reminder of happier times before you got down to work. You must be immensely proud of that.'

The blood rose in the cabbie's cheeks.

'Are you 'aving me on, mate?'

Sensing that the interview was not going well, Warbytton tried a different tack.

'Many perch and pike these days?' he asked.

The rot had set in a few years before. Disaffected with the usual run of faceless politicians, voters had installed a gaggle of single-issue campaigners, protesters, exhibitionists, stand-up comedians and oddballs in council chambers throughout the land. Advocates of haggis (Midlothian), fish and chips (Northumberland) and cream teas (Cornwall) were cousins under the skin to those representing body building (Stafford),

Friday

karaoke (Luton) and pole-dancing (Neasden). A pot-holer held the balance of power in Carlisle, while the Politically Correct Party had absolute control in Skegness and was bent on giving everyone a bracing time.

And now, Warbytton reflected, the circus animals were about to strut and prance in the Westminster ring, too. Perhaps even people like John Carrot.

'You don't stuff things,' he mused, sensing that something had gone wrong. He racked his memory bank. 'You're Double Glazers for Greater Government Transparency, perhaps?'

'I'm not.'

'Estate Agents Raising the Roof?'

'Do me a favour! Black Cabs Sounding Off for London.'

'Ah, of course.'

'Stands to reason, don't it? There's nobody talks to more people than us, so we've got our finger on the pulse, 'aven't we, and I can tell you what the people of London want – no, what they *don't* want, and that's governments telling them what to do, and what to eat, and how much exercise to take, and all that kind of gibberish, and don't even get me started on income bloody tax, taking money out of the pockets of those of us poor buggers trying to earn an honest living while the nobs at the top do nothin' but feather their own nests, because that's what it comes down to in the end, the rich get richer and the rest of us with sweated brows get less and less, except for all the free-loaders who sit on their arses and swill free handouts and all the ali babas who get off the boat and take our jobs given half the chance although they sure as hell won't get mine, because I tell you what, mate, there are those of us who won't take being messed about with, and when the nation can't take no more it'll be the black cab drivers who . . .'

It took a full five minutes to flag him down and ask the standard question: what was the deal?

Lady Thatcher's Wink

'Easy, ain't it? Shut down the tube network at nine o'clock every night.'

'So that . . .'

'Then everyone needs a taxi, right? See it as a reward for enterprise, the small man having a chance to get on.'

Warbytton, not having descended to the underground in years, had no idea at what time the last trains ran.

'We Need To Give This Serious Consideration,' he said solemnly.

The capitals this time were imprints on his brain from Turtle's powerpoint, slide 3, Essential Phrases. For some reason the fellow had an addiction to them.

'Labour are down for ten o'clock.'

'Although We Can Give No Hundredpercent Promise At This Moment In Time, It's An Idea Which Deserves Detailed Examination.'

'If that's your best offer,' the cabbie said, rising from his chair. 'Course, I'll have to see if I can improve on it elsewhere.'

'I Suggest We Continue to Keep All Lines of Communication Open . . . Sweet Jesus!'

'Beg pardon?'

But Warbytton had done with Carrot and fluttered his hand airily in dismissal. He had caught sight over the man's shoulder of a framed illustration on the wall – a bold caricature of Margaret Thatcher given on permanent loan to Number Ten by a well-wisher – and was shocked by the background detail. Had he never properly examined it before?

It was a friendly portrayal, the manic effect of those startlingly bright eyes softened by a flowing mane and a smile that stopped a little short of malevolence. The former premier stood before a stylised Big Ben with, or *once* with, the sketchiest suggestion of Parliament Square greensward stretching behind her.

Friday

Except that now she only had to look over her shoulder to witness an entwined couple, naked and athletically rutting.

*

Gerry Turtle swept along Oxford Street, marvelling with unashamed smugness at the gaudy splashes of orange and green blazoned in the afternoon sunlight on every fourth or fifth passer-by.

'Stands to reason . . .' his minicab driver was saying.

Those natty bibs (or *gilets*, as he liked to call them) were all his doing, albeit tactfully introduced as the inspiration of a grateful home secretary whose assault on the poor had finally exhausted the thesaurus. Just as the Department of Benefits had evolved into the Welfare Section and thence the Office of Handouts, so the unemployed had become the idle and then the workshy before transmogrifying into the feckless. ('Underclass' was held in readiness, but apparently the focus groups weren't quite ready for it.)

There, for some weeks, the campaign had stalled, until Turtle's brilliant, nay vivid, translation of verbal humiliation into visual. Make society's spongers, he gently suggested, sport glaring orange tokens of their shame.

'They're pathetic, isn't it?' the driver exploded into his speaking tube, appearing to be talking out of the back of his head. He waved an arm from his open window. 'So many who won't lift a finger . . .'

'While the rest of us . . .' Turtle prompted.

'. . . give the sweat of our brows . . .'

Turtle thumped the leatherette seat beside him with a triumphant punch as they swung into Langham Place. What a magician he was! The trick had been to find a slogan to lift the proud but humble worker above the feckless. Varieties of

Lady Thatcher's Wink

'sweated brow' had been written into ministerial speeches for weeks, and now it was on every lip. This would surely become known in future PR textbooks as the sweaty election.

'But not sweated *labour*,' he had instructed carefully. 'No mention of the opposition, and no suggestion of servitude.'

The plastic fashion accessories, as his more whimsical colleagues described them, had originally been proposed as compulsory outdoor wear for anyone receiving government benefits. (Policing them in the home was, unhappily, not yet feasible.) Go-getting clothing companies had queued up to promote their designs, and their waterproof nature gave rise to a suggested 'Gob on a gilet' slogan only narrowly defeated in Cabinet on the grounds that the 'g' was soft.

The opposition, terrified of seeming to sympathise with the downtrodden, nevertheless made a token protest, pointing out that most recipients of official largesse did have jobs, however meagre, and were therefore somewhat less feckless than the rest: they should be allowed to wear lime-green vests which, although they also sported the large H for Handouts on one shoulder, showed that their owners were at least a cut above their workless neighbours.

Turtle, as ever, had the last word. The government bill that swiftly passed into law accepted the two-colour divide but added bold blue stripes to the bibs, one for each of a wearer's onerous children guilty of draining the exchequer.

Now he skipped with improbable agility from the cab, ostentatiously tipped the still blabbering driver, grabbed his receipt and strode into the lobby of Broadcasting House.

'Mr Turtle,' acknowledged the doorman, the merest hint of 'yet again' in his tone.

Before he reached the lift, two familiar figures stepped out of it. The taller was a strapping woman in her early thirties, business dressed in dark jacket and trousers, a crimson silk

Friday

scarf spilling with assertive confidence over a crisp white blouse.

'The gorgeous Gloria!' he murmured.

'The gelatinous Gerry,' she countered, reaching forward to straighten his tie.

She had in tow an inoffensive looking grey-suited creature who straightened his own tie, as if in sympathy, and returned Turtle's scarcely perceptible nod.

'Two points ahead this morning,' she exulted.

'But not, I think you'll find, in the marginals.'

'Where trust in the Tories is down by three per cent.'

'And Labour is plumb bottom of the sexiest candidates ratings.'

Incessant chaffing had always been their métier, from those carefree fettuccine salad days reporting for the *Ham & High* to the subsequent path-crossing jaunts on a range of Fleet Street papers where their joshing intimacy had often set loose tongues wagging.

'Or perhaps I should say plump bottom,' Turtle added, avoiding the eye of her somewhat overweight companion.

Who would have thought, in those innocent times, that they would one day be jousting for the very future of the nation?

'Flying solo?' she asked him.

'You avoid the cock-ups if you do it yourself.'

'Don't tell me!'

'Sorry, sorry, sorry,' the grey suit broke in. 'Shouldn't have mentioned . . .'

'Enough, Alan!' Gloria yelped, seizing his elbow and beginning to tug him away. 'Too late for apologies now.'

'Something about Russia,' he mumbled abjectly to Turtle.

'Mere trivia, Alan,' she insisted, but Turtle had slipped a mobile from his top pocket and was thumbing his way through a slew of messages.

Lady Thatcher's Wink

'What you actually said,' he drawled, 'was that, and I quote, any more of their provocative flag-waving in freedom-loving Uzbekistan and we'll give Ivan a bazooka up his kremlin.'

'Oh, God! *Did* I?'

'Dear God, you did,' she confirmed.

He lowered his face into his hands and seemed to shrink.

'But I don't think we'll bother with that one, Gloria,' Turtle beamed over his bowed head. 'Unless you want to move away from the domestics. We're happier on home ground in these closing stages, aren't we?'

'That's where the votes are, Gerry.'

'Agreed, then.'

They high-fived with ironic, post-modern ostentation.

'It's just a question,' he said, 'of keeping the wretched troops on message.'

As his sparring partner led the contrite Leader of His Majesty's Loyal Opposition outside to blink sadly in the bright May sunshine, Turtle stepped into a basement-bound lift and was soon installed in front of a needy microphone.

'Sweaty weather,' he began.

*

A mile away to the south the Excalibur party was on the march, swarming under Admiralty Arch into the Mall, and Titch Tupper of the *Daily Excess*, famed as the smallest photographer on Fleet Street, was cursing the weight of his stepladder.

St George's flags fluttered in the sky over the bobbing heads above him, for all the world as if in progress towards the infidel walls of Acre, while several banners sporting a carefully photoshopped visage of the monarch (the monk-like tonsure digitally combed over) proclaimed the movement's motto FOR COUNTRY – AND KING, and an especially large specimen,

Friday

demanding two stout bearers for each timber support, villified its sworn enemies:

SCOTS
CYMRU
ULSTER
MIGRANTS

In case the last of these lacked clarity (SCUI wouldn't have done at all) someone had scrawled alongside it in broad crimson brush strokes *from abroad*.

Of course there were no papers on Fleet Street any more, and nobody had been called Titch for a couple of generations, but the diminutive snapper was one of the great survivors – less because of his talent (not a soul in this swelling throng lacked a device for taking a decent shot and sending it whizzing through the ether to a newsdesk), than because he had in a tin box safely stored under his bed a detailed print of the *Excess*'s careless proprietor, Viscount Macklethorpe, flash-bulbed in delicto amoroso with his secretary on the boardroom table. Tupper would either die in the job or retire – it was about time – with a gilt-edged pension.

Horribly hot and damp under the collar, he valiantly kept pace with the leaders of the procession until they arrived at last outside the gates of Buckingham Palace. The mood was festive, the busbied guards resignedly allowing show-offs to pose alongside them with gurning faces. He was about to open the legs of his ladder when it was rudely snatched from his grasp with a cry of 'Thanks, mate! Just the job if you don't mind.'

He did mind, as it happened, but the cry of protest died in his throat. The usurper was none other than the Excalibur founder and unassailable leader, Monty Muckle, an arrant rogue eulogised in an *Excess* leader this very morning as 'the man destined to return pride to the English'. He had brought a soapbox along to raise him above his audience – it lay between them now, its slats cracked from much use these last few weeks – but with customary go-gettedness had seized the lucky chance of a more commanding perch.

'I'm from the *Excess*,' Tupper offered lamely from below, but he was comfortably ignored.

Muckle exploded into sudden fury. The country was rotten, its native people were under threat and it was time to return to ancient values. He failed to mention King Arthur, but that was the general idea. A muscle-bound chancer in his thirties, he had been a stunt man, a chicken sexer, an all-in wrestler, a nightclub bouncer, a hotrod racer, a hospital porter, a car dealer and a barrow boy (and sometimes more than one of them at a time) before becoming a City trader and making enough money to throw his weight and his opinions around.

'We're strangers in our own country!' he bellowed.

'Excalibur!' they responded.

'This septic isle . . .' he foamed, but sensed that he had got something wrong and changed tack. 'The country of William Shakespeare. Albion!'

'Albion!' they chorused, though some were confused by the apparent football reference, and hardly any had heard or read a word of the Bard. 'Albion!'

The exchanges continued at full pelt for what felt like hours until after a prolonged celebratory chant of 'For country and king, for country and king!' there was an excited commotion in a part of the crowd which had a good view of the Palace.

A sudden still silence was followed by a fervent Nuremberg roar as the thoughtful monarch stepped forward on his balcony and flourished them a condescending wave.

*

Friday

Wot do these politishuns hope to know?

So began the evening blog. The world was waiting. Within seconds they would be arguing, abusing, cheering him on, spiralling off into fantasies of their own.

Hev dey ever spent a day in the real world, man? Do they know and feel what you and me know and feel? Freak, no!

Taz was, he liked to say, third generation street. That covered the case with as much information as anyone needed to know. The detail was big city routine: Indian grandfather settles in London after the war, marries a working-class English girl and sires a raven-haired, sallow-skinned son; the boy grows up to take an Anglo-Turkish wife and in turn produces a son of his own, whose exotic bloodline proves to be merely commonplace: he spends his schooldays (decent grades, never pushing for honours) among skin, hair and eyes of every human shade, daily deciphering a babel of sixty languages and more.

Street? Well, that was his affectation. Never mind that he'd been working dutifully at his father's carpet import business since his teens, in spirit he was down there among the brothers, effortlessly lacing a careless demotic with dashes of rude boy, rap and rasta. And the blog talk was a weird argot all his own.

Are dey worth a jog to the pol-ling stashun nex Thurs to earn a mark aginst their sorry names? Uh-HUH, bro!

It was the police that had made him, and one beefy, button-eyed individual in particular. Before that he was plain Emre, a nondescript, offwhite kid with no story to tell, but on the night of the demo he had been obliterated and reborn. All praise, then,

Lady Thatcher's Wink

to slow-witted, fired-up, gung-ho constable Ben Strutters who, looking for someone to harm, had spotted a slim, potentially vulnerable figure handily detached from the body of the march and had blundered forward with his Taser gun to wreak justice and inflict pain.

The bemused Emre, fresh out of his day's shift at the carpet warehouse and hardly aware of the HUNGER KILLS and FEED OUR CHILDREN banners waving around his head, saw the weapon advance towards him and experienced for a split second the joyous, abandoned buzz of an acid hit, all fizz and dream, before the electrodes scrambled his brain entirely and he collapsed senseless to the ground.

His death and resurrection had instantly become the stuff of legend. Bundled with no discernable heartbeat into an ambulance, he woke, pleasantly groggy, in a hospital bed, from which he offered a news agency cameraman (artfully disguised in surgeon scrubs) a weak smile and two raised thumbs.

Who was he? A villain to the *Daily Maul* and similar sheets of establishment bent, who quoted poor Strutters, a grievously wronged public servant forced to defend himself against 'a savage beast, charging at me like a wild bull'. His would-be assailant had 'bristled with menace' and had singled him out for what was on the point of becoming a vicious assault, 'all the time mouthing a string of obscenities you wouldn't hear outside the navy'. (Strutters, having never set foot on a ship, had a possibly unjust opinion of the senior service.) His enemy had then put a hand in his pocket, for all the world as if to produce a gun or a knife, giving the shaking constable – 'I was, frankly, terrified!' – no option but to raise his own puny weapon in self defence.

THE SMIRKING SAINT ran the *Maul* headline, alongside the hospital photograph.

Friday

Here's the smug face of one of the unpatriotic do-gooders who threatened our brave police yesterday while championing the increasing droves of useless people unable to provide their kids with three decent meals a day.

The bleeding hearts swarmed outside buildings in the City of London, obstructing financiers attempting to go about their vital work on behalf of the nation.

But to others, he was a victim swiftly elevated to the rank of hero. His father, though loathing the publicity, nevertheless felt bound to explain what a model son he had ever been ('a joy to his mother's heart'), while a score of protesters and onlookers usefully sent the more amenable newspapers colourful snaps and videos of the incident. These presented a physical image of the newly christened 'Taser Boy', all twenty-four years of him, in a more or less flattering light, depending on one's point of view – not so much a muscular, testosterone fuelled lion as a mild, dainty-footed gazelle.

'Wouldn't pull the wings off a fly,' added his father, whose command of English colloquialism was less than perfect.

The cynosure of every cynical PR eye, Taser Boy became the poster boy for the hard-done-by, of whom there happened to be rather a lot. His hitherto lame blog, shared with a few old friends, became a must-read for hundreds, then thousands, then tens of thousands. Writing as Taz, he at first concentrated on matters surrounding his canonisation – how it felt to be Tasered, the protest movement he had stumbled upon, Ben Strutters' commendation and promotion – but there was no diminishing of his celebrity status as he began to stray far beyond his feeble area of knowledge and competence.

When dem politicos come a-knockin on your door, frenz, tell em we'll be knockin hard on theirs tomorrow.

Lady Thatcher's Wink

He wasn't sure what that meant, but it had a tingle of threat about it that he liked.

Come the revolushun . . .

But his own door had opened downstairs, and the delectable Chloe was calling up to him: 'Are we going out or not?'

He scrubbed the last line, hit the send button and replied in polite, almost submissive, tones his audience would have utterly failed to recognise as in-your-face Taz-speak.

SATURDAY

'You're late again, Applied Mathematics!'

It was, indeed, two minutes past five in the morning, and the brisk Daphne was having none of it.

'That pathetic excuse for a vehicle,' she exclaimed chirpily as a distraught young man lurched among them, 'is nothing but a false economy.'

She bustled to a chart on the wall, took up a marker pen and splodged an indictment against his name. It was the third.

The crippled offender staggered into the centre of the room clutching a unicycle with a dramatically bent wheel. There was blood on his forehead and on the tip of his extravagant blond quiff, one arm hung heavily from the shoulder as if numb and his jogging trousers were torn at the knees.

'Can't control the bloody thing!' he exploded.

'Martin!' cried one of the girls, stepping forward with a damp J-cloth, and dabbing it at the cut. (The grim apparition of a failed circus performer was the only male among them.) 'What on earth happened?'

'Don't you be showing him any sympathy, Anthropology Two,' Daphne rebuked her cheerfully. 'Didn't I always say it was asking for trouble? That's one pound fifty he's been docked in a week.'

'It's just a couple of minutes,' protested another of the girls, taking a ruthless sponge to his grazed elbow. 'Nobody has to know.'

'Dishonest to a fault, Media Studies,' chided the implacable Daphne with a twinkle in her eye. 'Once I start breaking the rules, Power4Us will have me in the jobs queue before I can squeeze the suds from a mop.' She looked warily about her. 'There's probably a camera,' she added.

Daphne might be unrelenting in her application of their terms of employment, but she undeniably had a soft spot for her captive cleaning team. What glorious innocents they all were! It seemed only yesterday that she had been herding flocks of silent, abashed, Latvian, Namibian and Uzbeki workers around government offices, hardy survivors of life's calamities with little English and few expectations. Now that the Britons First Act placed immigrants below native-born applicants in the jobs queue her little workforce had a different composition altogether.

'Time to go, my darlings!' she called, hearing the minibus draw up outside.

The abject Martin deposited his stricken rim alongside a gaggle of regular bicycles and silently wished Power4Us in the nether regions of hell. That happy outcome would, he had to admit, bring the entire nation to its knees, since the company was the provider of every last outsourced government service, from tax collection to the criminal courts (air traffic control was this very week in the process of being handed over), but he felt prepared to accept the consequences, however grim.

After all, had he not so recently been a keen and elegant practitioner, weaving his way among the city traffic with all the deftness of a sempstress's needle? Yes, he had grumbled about having to pay the company twenty pence a day for storing his bike during working hours – and had been fined for his insolence under a little-known 'public dissension' rule – but that seemed a blessed period of his life now. As more and more of the less able-bodied were forced into work the company had seized on a surge in the use of tricycles and mobility scooters to devise a lucrative 'ten pence per wheel' levy instead. Whereas the frail, unbalanced and legless had little option but to cough up, the fit, adventurous and broke knew what they had to do: unicycling had become the biggest rage since hoola hoops.

Saturday

'Chemical Engineering, Media Studies and Anthropology One to the Foreign Office. Applied Mathematics, Early Modern History and Anthropology Two to Downing Street.'

Not a single member of Daphne's family had ever been to university, and she shuddered to think that her grandchildren would ever give it a second thought. Far better to manage them than to join them. As for the roll-call of their degrees, well, that was her little joke. An earlier generation had commonly rechristened the servants to suit their own convenience.

'Tourist Management, Pharmacology, Maritime Law and Earth Sciences to the Department of Education. Now *that* should lift your flagging spirits . . . '

*

If Alan Sprout had ever experienced greater pain he couldn't remember it. The incessant pricking of the needles in his chest was certainly the worst torture he had ever volunteered for, although, in the circumstances, that was hardly the correct verb to use.

'How much more?' he pleaded, his fists clenched, his eyes screwed tight, his forehead beaded with sweat under the lights. He lay supine on a padded fake-leather bench, stripped to the waist.

'Nearly there,' chimed the implacable Gloria, taking a turn around the room to examine the fantasy artwork on show. It was their third early morning visit, the parlour's curtains drawn, the regular clientele not yet arrived for their bravely borne surgical adornments. 'Don't make such a fuss, Alan.'

It was his tortured brain that had made the fuss in the dark hours before dawn, plunging him into a luridly lit dungeon of writhing forms, glistening scales and fantastically flexed muscles, all in vibrant tones of vermilion, viridian green, citrus yellow, bruised purple, flamingo pink, cobalt blue. He woke thrashing in soaking sheets that were gloriously, innocently white.

'Ten minutes, mate,' muttered the ministering Youssef, bent low over him, his aftershave a strange, cloying mixture of candied peel and coconut. 'We almost done, mister. Unless I persuade you to add a little dragon, maybe?'

This was the proprietor's running joke, and it was wearing thinner than his multi-coloured inks.

'You lucky to have some extra flesh,' he added. 'Hurts a bit more if you skinny fellow.'

Gloria, less than comradely, laughed uproariously at this notion.

Sprout had never been one for show. When his friends at the car works grew moustaches or sported earrings he was solid old Al who got on with things and never caused a stir. Then he was their solid union rep, who stuck to his guns and learned which strings to pull. And then he was a councillor, and next he was an MP. And now, to his eternal surprise, he was the leader of the opposition.

Youssef tapped him on the shoulder with a stubby finger, evidently a signal of dismissal.

'No dragons, no hearts, no arrows,' he said. 'All finished. It is, how I think you say, a labour of love. *Labour*, no?'

'Ha, ha,' Sprout said flatly.

'It looks splendid,' Gloria enthused, producing a credit card.

'Best thing,' Youssef added, as they prepared to leave. 'Your skin a bit folded, know what I mean, so best display with the chest extended, your arms out wide.'

He demonstrated.

'Like a crucifixion,' Sprout said.

*

Saturday

Jessica Warbytton would not be budged by wheedling, special pleading, crude threat or insult.

'We have a full weekend on here, Eggie,' she instructed her husband, cradling the telephone between firm jaw and shoulder as she zipped up her jodphurs. Through the oriel window a vision of springy turf stretched away enticingly between an overhang of verdant trees. 'Couldn't possibly come up to town. Quite out of the question.'

'But you promised.'

'When?'

'Not when, but who – Gerry Turtle. As he's just reminded me.'

'Ha! Any deal made with your Galapagos reptile should *on principle* be regarded as immediately null and void.'

'This blasted election is only days away and he says it's vital we appear as a unit.'

'A *what*?'

'That's how he talks. Husband and wife and all that. Family.'

'You don't even like being prime minister, Eggie.'

'But I have to pretend that I do. He calls it semblance.'

'It's such an odious waste of your time. You could be worming the spaniels.'

'Please!'

'Why not come up here and make a stirring speech or two?'

'Because London is what he calls the battleground. Dozens of marginal seats. I have to be here.'

'And that cramped bear-pit of a second bedroom at Number Ten! You wouldn't squeeze an orphan child in there, or even let it out to a –'

'No, we don't say darkie any more, Jessie. And Downing Street isn't on the rentals market as far as I'm aware. You could share mine at a pinch.'

'Have you forgotten what happened last time we slapped up in the same bed?'

'*Freddie!*' they both exclaimed at once.

'And there's your answer, old cock,' Jessica said abruptly, with the air of a cardsharp vanquishing his ace of spades with a two of trumps. 'I'll send Freddie down. He needs to get away. Touch of the usual girl trouble, plus some imminent law and order issues, as they seem to call them these days.'

Warbytton groaned.

'Couldn't possibly work,' he said. 'Bullingdon's horribly out of favour these days, Jessie. Respectability's in.'

'Nonsense. I'll pack him off in the Rover tomorrow. He'll enjoy a bit of London buzz.'

'One of the girls, perhaps? Veronica's graceful.'

'But she's just been appointed high sheriff, Eggie. Far too busy. She's opening our spring fête this afternoon and I've got her down for WI duty next week.'

'High sheriff? She's hardly out of school.'

'Twenty-eight, Eggie, at the last count, as perhaps you ought to know. Truth is, I couldn't think of anyone else to put up for it. *Noblesse oblige.*'

'Diana, then.'

'Far too risky from your point of view. She's going through one of her unstable interludes.'

'The born-agains again?'

'That's over. Failed to catch someone who keeled over in an ecstatic trance and divine rapture became double rupture. Some unChristian sentiments were expressed, I believe.'

'Mindfulness, then?'

'Too good at it. Kept falling asleep through meal times, and you know how she enjoys a healthy tuck-in. Woke relaxed but furiously ravenous. Goodness knows where the Buddha got all that flesh. No, she's gone all political.'

Saturday

'Good God, that's awful. Tory, I assume?'

'I hardly think so. She brought a weedy young man to supper last night who's canvassing for the Freeloaders Alliance. At least, I think that's what he called it. Perhaps it was Teetotal on second thoughts, because he wouldn't touch a drop. Something tiresomely worthy, whatever it may be. And Diana's sponsored a porker in this afternoon's pig races and called it Trotsky. So I'm afraid it has to be the son and heir, Eggie.'

'No, please not Freddie,' Warbytton expostulated with as much minatory animation as his embattled spirit could muster. 'Keep him away from here, Jessie. I absolutely forbid it.'

He was uncertain whether the last sound he heard before the line went dead was pitiless laughter or one of the horses whinnying in the stables.

*

The opinion polls were all aquiver. One had the Conservatives on 25 per cent, with Labour a point behind, Excalibur and Others tied on 18 per cent, narrowly ahead of Don't Know (15 per cent). Another reversed the position of the two leading parties, promoted Don't Know to 25 per cent, demoted Excalibur to a poor fourth and declared the rest hardly worth thinking about.

TORIES STRIDING TO VICTORY! trumpeted the *Maul*; LABOUR ON A SURGE! triumphed the *Blither*; ENGLAND SPEAKS! trilled the *Excess*; and scarcely anyone read them.

*

Ellie Stammers thought she might be in love. Whatever it was, she knew that Greg Gripp was the most commanding man she had ever come across since the bailiff who turfed her mother and her squealing little brood out on to the streets all those years ago. She gazed at him now through the double-strength security glass as he rounded up what he merrily called 'the runners' for his 11.30 handicap (with relentless cajoling and badgering they managed to fit two into an hour). She was rather proud of her green bib, which proved that at least she was trying to be a decent citizen, but Gripp wore a pinstriped suit and a large flapping tie bearing the Power4Us logo. He was in charge, and he stood no nonsense. He was wonderful.

What a privilege it was to work here. The carved stone windows, dark oak beams and parquet flooring were reminders of the days when this was one of those borough libraries long since sold off for more profitable use. Perhaps it was nothing more than the lingering waft of ancient furniture polish, but although the fittings had been stripped out to suit the demands of the Office of Handouts' Rigorous Assessment Unit, and although she had never been much of a reader herself, Ellie was convinced that, in moments of quietness, she still sensed a trace of an imagined dusty, studious, intellectual atmosphere. It was uplifting.

Having marshalled his sorry looking field of claimants into a starting line, Gripp strode to the far end of the room, took a ten-pound note from his pocket and taped it to the wall.

"We're looking for strivers, remember,' he announced. 'We want to see real effort. First to the end gets the prize.'

He popped his head into Ellie's little booth.

'Ready?' he asked.

She held up her stop-watch in assent.

'Good girl. There are ten runners and we've an eighty per cent target today, so you can work that out?'

Maths had always taxed her brain, but this seemed doable.

'We send two away,' she offered after some thought.

Saturday

'Wrong, Ellie. We send eight away. It's a *refusal* target. You'll learn,' he added generously before rejoining his charges.

And now for the performance that she always enjoyed with a shiver of guilt, though she couldn't quite say why. It felt a bit naughty, to tell the truth, as if she might be caught out smiling to herself and scolded, though there was nobody to see. It was their little secret.

'They're all ready for the off,' Gripp declared, in the breezy tones of a professional race commentator. 'In the stall to my left' (of course there was no stall, but excitable Ellie pictured one nevertheless), 'we have Diabetes One with restricted leg movement, but a definite will to win. Next to her, champing at the bit, is Emphysema, a bit choked up but ready for the fray. Next, it's Pneumo . . . how do you say that?'

'Pneumoconiosis,' wheezed an elderly chap, holding his chest. 'Look, I'm not sure I can go through with this.'

'Nonsense,' Gripp chafed him. 'You look a hell of a lot better than I did when I fell out of bed after a few tinnies last Sunday morning! It's Pneumo Lad, and then we have Hippy Girl, three weeks after the operation and grumbling a bit, but nothing that a flick of the whip won't put right. Or is your money perhaps on Heart Bypass Boy, carrying brand new stents?'

Ellie thought he was a real card. It was so impressive, the way he improvised from the few details he had on his sheet. It was such a pity that none of them seemed to appreciate it. Where was their sense of humour?

'Fresh out of her wheelchair it's Arthritic Knees, bunched up with Bell's Palsy and Curvature of the Spine – not sure that's one to *back*, folks! And on the rails we have the very game Double Hernia, by Too Much Straining out of Carelessness, jostling for position with Colostomy Kate. They're under starter's orders.'

Her thumb hovered expectantly over the stopwatch button.

Lady Thatcher's Wink

'Ready... steady... (he approached the booth, handed her the sheet and gave her a massive knowing wink)... 'hobble!'

They set off, slowly, erratically, pausing to catch breath, to clutch at a limb or to cough. After only a few staggering paces the man with the lung disease clutched his heart and fell to the floor, motionless, toppling the woman with the hip replacement. She sat down heavily and raised her hands for help, but all the others were struggling forward in laboured desperation, their limbs seeming to wade through treacle.

'Two riders are down,' Gripp enthused in his breathless track commentator's voice. 'It's looking like a photo between Hernia and Curvature. But here comes Colostomy Kate lurching up on the outside...'

'Should we call an ambulance?' Ellie asked. 'He hasn't moved.'

'Could be faking it,' he said before raising his voice again. 'But no, it's Curvature holding on with the finishing line in sight. Oh, he's *bent* on victory...'

It was obvious that he was dead. Two of her uncles had gone like that, straight down and without even the ghost of a gasp or a tremor. She crossed his name off the list: only seven left to go.

When the race was over Gripp handed the winner his tenner, asking Ellie to record that it should be offset against any future benefits, and wished him a courteous farewell.

'But haven't I passed the test?' the stooped figure asked, pocketing the note. 'Didn't I strive? Look at this sweat!'

'Pass me the sheet, please, Ellie,' Gripp said. He glanced at the figures. 'One minute 14 seconds, Mr Rosejoy. You're an athlete.'

'You mean...'

'In short, you're feckless. You come here expecting hand-outs when you can cross this room in little more than a minute. You're very lucky indeed to be striding out – practically

Saturday

sprinting, I'd say – with ten pounds in your pocket. I could have you arrested.'

'And what about the rest of us?' demanded the woman with the colostomy bag. 'I got knocked over.'

'The question is whether that was a tactical ruse or not,' he mused. 'After due consideration I'm prepared to give you another chance. Come back next month.'

'But what do I do in the meantime? I'm broke.'

'Go home and practise your mobility, Mrs Pardew. The purpose of this exercise is to create a fair world for all, and in particular for those who keep people like you in food and drink.'

At this moment two medics wearing green vests over their uniform stepped into the room, lifted the dead body on to a stretcher and hurried out again.

'It's lucky for one of you that Mr Cathcart dropped out,' Gripp said. He consulted the sheet again. 'Our cut-off time today is one minute 55 seconds. Emphysma and Bell's Palsy can sign on. The rest of you can go home.'

'My neighbour clocked 1.45 last week,' the heart patient said, 'and he's got a handout.'

'That was last week.'

'But this is completely arbitrary!'

'It's not arbitrary,' Gripp said. 'It's my decision.'

How masterful he was, Ellie thought, and how generous. Only six of these orange bibs had been completely turned away, unless you counted Mr Cathcart, and of course you couldn't.

*

The taxidermist had reassuringly soft hands, with the bonus of beautifully manicured nails. After he had bowed himself out

Lady Thatcher's Wink

with fitting obsequiousness, Warbytton allowed himself the luxury of taking in the Thatcher portrait once again.

'Sweet Jesus,' he exhaled, in unconscious self-parody.

For the unknown artist had been at it again. A tree had magically sprung up behind the tussling couple on the lawn, its stout trunk a convenient support for another display of brute concupiscence. Fleshy parts of a female form espaliered against the bark like a tamed quince were tantalisingly glimpsed beyond the bulk of her large and hairy lover, who, stooping to his business, presented to the viewer a huge, fleshy, and protuberant rump.

*

The easterly bound traffic in Piccadilly had slowed to a crawl and was already backing up several blocks thanks to a troupe of eight green-vested unicyclists who, expertly shifting in their saddles as if plagued by a relentless dose of the itch, hefted a huge LET THE PEOPLE SPEAK banner that stretched the width of the thoroughfare.

'I wonder what that means,' said a woman distracted from her window-shopping outside Fortnum & Mason.

'Must be a political slogan of some sort,' her companion guessed. 'It doesn't have to mean anything.'

'I'd like to know, though.'

Encamped under the statue of Eros, a youth pathetically armed with nothing but a puny bow and arrow, Inspector Ben Strutters and his team of uniformed heavies prepared their mightier arsenal for the coming scrap. After frisking all potential witnesses for their cameras and mobiles under the conveniently ambiguous Police Sanctity Act, they had efficiently cleansed Piccadilly Circus of its milling riffraff and now eagerly lay in wait for the enemy.

Saturday

'First, tear gas in the eyes,' Strutter instructed. 'Next, batons to the wrists. I want to *hear* the contact. If any of them get up and advance, then it's the Tasers. Any questions?'

'Yes, sir,' stammered a nervous constable. 'What if members of the public get in the way?'

Strutter brought his face up close.

'You down them, PC Dunnock,' he said, 'with as much force as you consider necessary. Perhaps a little bit more. There *is* no general public, remember. This is war.'

Unhappily, these worthy public order defences were not to be put to the test. Back in Piccadilly, as pedestrians stepped smartly on to the pavement to make way for the advancing juggernaut, they exposed (far too late for the nearest rider to take avoiding action) a step-ladder that had been unfolded, with reckless neglect, on the edge of the road. In the ensuing mighty crash, its diminutive occupant was toppled to the ground, where he lay, wrapped in the folds of the tangled banner, alongside a team of bruised and bleeding cyclists.

'Utter carnage,' the window shopper said. 'I do hope that camera's insured.'

*

Come the revolushun . . .

Taz had Saturday afternoons off, and he didn't need all the free hours before his evening's bacchanalia to primp, to preen and to prod his slack stomach into tight pants, as he inevitably termed them. (Trousers were for yesterday's people.) It was blog time, if only he had something to say.

. . . what are you and me gonna be elbowin the future for, frenz? When dey look up, what will dey see comin for em?

In truth, he hadn't a clue, although he supposed it ought to be something better than working in a carpet warehouse.

So you tell me, citizens of de world . . .

he thumped the keyboard, passing the buck,

. . . and together let's confabulate our own unique and hi-cred people's manifesto!

He was rather proud of 'confabulate', but the adorable Chloe, arriving unexpectedly early and leaning over his shoulder to read it, pulled a face.

'You need some new material,' she said.

*

'So sorry to drag you over on a Saturday evening,' Gerry Turtle smiled thinly, 'but we thought we ought to clear the air a little, didn't we, Bodge?'

'Oh, certainly,' Justin Bodgers nodded severely, sitting upright in his armchair to indicate high seriousness. 'Especially at this delicate juncture.'

'Delicate juncture,' Turtle breathed in assent. As it was his own suggested phrase, it was certainly worth repeating, and with some relish. He, playing a different role, sank back into a leather cushioned embrace, crossing his legs to show a pair of surprisingly bright blue socks. 'Couldn't have put it better myself.'

'Let's just get on with it,' said the occupant of a third chair, studiously ignoring the large scotch on the rocks that had been deposited with a flourish on a table in front of him. 'Deliver your party piece and I'll be off home.'

Saturday

'Tch, tch, let's not be aggressive, Terry,' Turtle frowned. He lowered his voice to a stage whisper and brought his hands in front of his chest, surreptitiously indicating behind him with this thumbs. 'We're being recorded, don't forget.'

'Yes, I am familiar with cameras. No doubt too familiar as far as you're concerned.'

'It's what you do with them,' Bodgers said. 'That's the issue, isn't it?'

Terry Bolt was for a moment back in the prep school where all three of them had first met. The dynamic, as Turtle would no doubt call it, was unchanged: preening Gerry the smart arse, stolid Bodge the teacher's pet, himself wanting out.

'Evidence,' he said flatly.

'Meaning?'

'You're about to accuse us of bias, so let's have the facts.'

The little twitch of Turtle's lips alerted him to his mistake, but it was too late. It was almost too late for the BBC itself, which had been starved of funds and half dismantled, its enemies beckoned in for the kill. Bolt had the mundane title head of news, but was universally known to sympathetic colleagues as the decidedly uppercase Head in Noose. He certainly wanted out.

'What about the platform you've given to trade union leaders?' Bodgers said, producing a large ring-binder crammed with documents. He extricated a sheet, waved it in the air and ran a forefinger down the lines. 'Fifteen minutes and twelve seconds in the past month alone.'

'This is a crime?'

'Not yet, though I understand it's being worked on.'

Bodgers of course loved his own capital letters, of which, after a career doing nothing much in the law and then making up the numbers on countless lucrative committees, he had an

Lady Thatcher's Wink

impressive array. The relevant ones here were Neutrality Overseer, Broadcasting, a post created a year ago and which he had filled with bristling vigour.

'The leader of the opposition once ran a union,' Bolt reminded him.

'*Once*, Terry,' the NOB wagged his head sagely. 'You surely don't think for a moment that he'd dare speak up in favour of unions today. Remember Clement Attlee? Remember Jeremy Corbyn? Labour tried socialism once and flirted with it a second time before they finally learned their lesson. The British people like to appear bolshy from time to time, but they really crave being led by their betters. Ask the House of Windsor.'

'And the oddballs . . .' Turtle prompted.

'Yes, you do seem fixated on the disruptive,' Bodgers said. 'The archbishop of Canterbury harping on about the homeless – five minutes, 24 seconds on all channels.'

'We always play devil's advocate,' Bolt countered drily, aware that the irony would founder.

'But it's the exposure, the very fact of giving airtime to subversive views. Have you read my brief?'

'A clever piece of work. Cunningly elastic.'

Turtle was unable to supress a self-congratulatory flush.

'You think so, Terry?' he beamed, before swiftly catching himself in the act and affecting a more seemly sneer. 'You don't think you have a duty of care to your susceptible listeners and viewers?'

'Four minutes, seven seconds given over to economists questioning austerity,' Bodgers continued. 'Second-rate economists, as my advisers have made clear. So-called experts. A piece about illegal immigrants rightly incarcerated in the new Bongo Bins, with inmates encouraged to criticise their treatment by Power4Us operatives – who are, in any case, nothing to do with the government.

Saturday

'Three interviews conducted with orange bibs in food banks, all making outrageous claims meant, I suppose, to bring tears to susceptible eyes. A charity for the disabled . . .'

'For disabled people,' Turtle corrected him, with a warning twitch towards the camera. 'It can be edited,' he murmured.

'A charity for disabled people, for a full two minutes, six seconds, allowed to suggest some vague kind of suffering allegedly caused by government measures – and without a minister on hand to refute it.'

'Probably declined to appear,' Bolt said shortly.

Bodgers fixed him with a pitying, almost kindly, gaze.

'Don't you think that in those circumstances, Terry, you should drop an interview? This is a democracy, remember. Two sides to every question. You make my job very difficult.'

'Have you read the right wing press lately?' Bolt came back, forgetting his intention not to be goaded. 'Two sides to every question?'

'Oh dear, that's a very old-fashioned line to take, Terry,' Turtle threw in. 'A category error, if I may say so. It's not right and left any more. And it's not class. That's all yesterday's talk. It's doers and won't be doing today. It's striving versus conniving. It's winning and losing.'

'And the papers don't concern me,' Bodgers added. 'Not my brief, remember. I'm charged with ensuring that the BBC reflects a reasonable status quo. Those are the very words. I take that as meaning a middle line, a common view. Doesn't that sound reasonable to you?'

'So where do you draw that middle line?' Bolt almost growled.

'Where would *you* draw it?'

'Haven't a clue.'

'That's all too evidently the case, Terry. Then let me suggest to you that it's very close to where the government draws it.

Lady Thatcher's Wink

The elected government of this country, after all. You don't need to wander very far to either side, especially with a general election only days away.'

Bolt stood up and, in a sudden explosion of defiance, addressed his frustration to the camera.

'I abjectly confess to shameful bias in the BBC's coverage,' he declared, opening his arms in a gesture of mock defeat. 'It's time for us to withdraw from political interviewing. From now on we'll concentrate on sport, gardening and weather forecasts.'

Bodgers seemed to give the idea serious consideration.

'It's the hottest May on record,' he said, 'and set to continue. You could make some interesting programmes on that. A great idea, Terry.'

'Which reminds me,' Turtle added, following him to the door. 'Your forecasters keep on and on about their humidity readings. That sounds horribly technical, Terry. Wouldn't it be more user-friendly if we changed it to the sweat count?'

*

The king, waking from a snooze on his private jet, checked his watch with disbelief.

'How long have we been up here, Roddy?'

'More than an hour, sir,' the pilot said over his shoulder. 'It's the first day for Power4Us in the control tower and they seem to be having trouble with the buttons. Nobody's heard me.'

'Is the bloody place manned?'

'Oh, I can hear *them* well enough, sir. Chap called Smithy enjoyed a ruddy good caper at the Beefcake Club last night.'

The monarch, an impatient man, pounded a fist against the fuselage.

'And Willo's tucking in to a bleedin' tasty cheese, chilli and tomato sandwich.'

SUNDAY

Sleep was impossible. Warbytton had woken at five, his window wide open against the heat, intermittent traffic noise already grumbling along Whitehall, a stupid fly beating its body against the pane before skimming his head and bouncing off the walls, a glimpse of blue sky warning of yet another stifling city day ahead. He thought lovingly of the green acres of home, of shade under the trees, of breakfast on the terrace, even of Jessie with her insufferable bounce.

It was no good. At six o'clock he swung himself out of bed, dashed his face with cold water, threw on an old shirt and some comfortable trousers, poked his feet into a battered and undemanding pair of leather slippers and set off on a tour of his temporary domain.

His destination was the room where he had greeted Turtle's army of demanding little shits and, more importantly, where a certain picture had begun repeatedly to visit his mind with the persistence of an obsession. Warbytton had never in all his life turned the leaves of a dirty book or watched a pornographic film, but he wondered a little guiltily, as he pushed open the door, whether his fascination with the evolving Thatcher portrait was entirely free of impropriety.

'Sweet Jesus!' he exclaimed yet again.

Perched on a high stool, a charcoal stick in her hand, was a young woman in a green bib who, working in oblivious concentration, was adding further touches to the work in question.

'Who on earth are you?' he asked.

She turned a pretty face towards him, surprised but by no means cowed.

'I'm Anthropology Two,' she said.

'You're what?'

'It's the way they name the cleaners. That was my degree at university. UCL. A high 2:1.'

He drew closer to inspect her fresh handiwork. How on earth had she managed that subtlety with just a few additional strokes? One of Mrs Thatcher's eyelids was now lowered in a gross wink, and a hint of suppressed amusement played along the slightest lifting of the corners of her mouth. The former premier was, the portrait now revealed, thoroughly aware of the athletic carnality being enjoyed behind her back. A viewer ignorant of her true character might even suspect that she had played procuress in bringing the two rampant couples together in the first place. Forget the Mona Lisa: this was closer to saucy seaside postcard.

Warbytton indicated the steatopygous buttocks of the satyr by the tree.

'These are South Sea Islanders?'

'They're who?'

'Isn't that what anthropologists study – strange native customs and all that? Depraved innocence?'

He was proud of himself for not mentioning darkies. She smiled, prettily.

'Bingo halls in Hackney, actually. "Your number's up: dissonances in cross-community validation, a semiological perspective." That was my thesis.'

'I see,' said Warbytton, who didn't.

'Are you going to report me?'

'I don't think so. But perhaps you'd better stop now.'

She produced a mobile phone and took a photograph of the portrait, holding it up to show him.

'It's finished anyway,' she said. 'Are you on the staff here?'

'I suppose I am in a way. I'm the prime minister.'

'Oh.'

Sunday

She looked at him long and hard.

'You're Freeman Goodblow.'

'He was the last one.'

'I don't follow these things much. Wasn't there a scandal – sex or money?'

'Both. And more. Everything you can imagine, in fact. One headline ran "Hands-in-till bigamist PM starved cats to death in sex torture den".'

'That sounds fun. Which particular crime did for him, then?'

'Oh, none of those. He'd have shrugged them off in the usual way, even the cats, but he made the mistake of calling a transgender MP him instead of her, or perhaps it was her instead of him (it was all hopelessly confusing), and that was a step too far. A pure accident, but we're very sensitive about gender in the Commons these days. He had to go.'

'So you're . . .'

'Sturgeon Warbytton.' He almost added 'at your service', because she did have the loveliest figure and the most winning smile. 'You can call me Warbie.'

'Thank you.'

'And this cleaning of yours. Is that more research?'

'It's not "cleaning", Warbie,' she instructed him, wagging quotation mark fingers around the word. 'It's cleaning. It's what I do for a sort of living.'

'But you're a university graduate . . .'

They regarded one another in mutual incomprehension.

'Surely you could be doing something better than this. Not, of course,' (Turtle's No Condescension rule suddenly dropped down from the Powerpoint bar) 'that I wish to belittle cleaners, Who Do Valuable Work for the Community.'

'I wanted to study art,' she said, 'but the government closed most of the colleges down.'

'Did they? I mean, did we?'

The slippers in particular were worrying her.

'Are you sure you're the prime minister?' she asked. 'You don't seem to know much about how things work.'

'Oh, I'm not that kind of prime minister,' he said. 'Not that kind of politician, really. I'm just minding the shop here until someone more suitable comes along. I hate the job, to be truthful, absolutely hate it. I'm given horrible speeches to make that I don't properly understand.'

'Poor Warbie. Why on earth did they give it to you?'

'Because I'm the opposite of Freeman Goodblow, essentially. I'm what they call a grandee. I simply mind my own business and don't bother with all this policy stuff. Never have. I'm happy to till my own furrow at Eggerton Manor – not literally, you understand – and pop down to London for an obedient vote every now and then.

'You'd adore the old house,' he found himself adding. 'Tudor, with a priest hole. Capability Brown landscape with two lakes. I'd love to show you around it.'

She laughed, showing, he thought, teeth like pearls.

'I'm sure our two worlds would clash horribly, Warbie,' she said, taking up a bucket and sponge and making to leave. 'You clearly don't know how the other half live.'

A giddy kind of release suddenly seemed to offer itself to him, a mental exploration that might transport him for a while from the certainties of Eggerton Manor but, more deliciously, beyond the fell clutches of Gerry Turtle.

'Please don't rush off,' he said. 'Tell me about it.'

*

Grate idea bout your peoples manifesto, Taz. Put me down for free weed, free love and free downloads. Lets all party!!!
tumbleweed647

Sunday

> Sign me up, Tazer Boy. First step, get rid of all those LYING POLITICIANS//*TS1 ALERT!* Let the people speak.
> *blackguardking*

> But youve bin telling us not to vote, you fugging idiot. Now you want a manifesto. Have you got a brain in your stupid head?
> *voyceofreezun*

> How to choose between DIRTY TORIES//*TS1 ALERT!*, corrupt lefties, feeble liberals, BUSINESSMEN ON THE MAKE//*TS1 ALERT!*, greedy trade unionists, workshy unemployed bastards, wingeing benefit scroungers, SINISTER SPOOKS//*TS2 ALERT!!* and Uzbeki immigrants with begging bowls? This countrys on its knees and its too late to do shit all about it – fact.
> *grumblebucket*

You couldn't look at your screen these days without the heavy block capitals of the Terrorism Suppression alerts flashing their warnings. The grade 1 'Citizen Advice' rebukes were so common as to be something of a joke, but they doubtless kept the more nervous in line. Grade 2 'State Aware' alerts stacked up against a sender's name until they reached danger level, although nobody knew how many hits it required to trigger a ring on the bell or an early-hours smashing down of the door. After a 'Red Light' Grade 3, it was commonly believed, you could expect a court appearance, almost certainly behind closed doors and without a jury.

> Arseholes of the world unite! Support the mighty Taz and swirl us all down the stinking sinkhole of history. Oh you bleeding useless jumped up lIttIe fool!
> *citygent*

There were hundreds of messages this morning, buzzing about his head like blowflies swarming from a bloated corpse,

Lady Thatcher's Wink

and he suddenly felt very weary. It wasn't that he cared about either the slapdash English (he was slovenly with spelling and apostrophes himself) or the omnipresent bile (he could dish out crude repartee with the worst of them). No, what was getting to Taz was the sheer tedious predictability of it all.

Chloe was right: he needed new material.

*

Alan Sprout's passion could no longer be delayed. His callous dominatrix had surprisingly allowed him a day to assimilate Youssef's physical and mental torment, but now here they were at Speakers' Corner, jostled by an impatient crowd and (how endless the day seemed already!) with a long and crippling Via Dolorosa stretching ahead of them.

'A brisk half an hour for the media shots and the Number Three speech,' Gloria prepared him in her no-nonsense way, 'and then we've a pretty full itinerary.' She glanced down at her clipboard. 'Barking, Brent, Chingford, Ruislip, Tooting . . .'

'Stations of the cross,' moaned Sprout, who'd had a Catholic upbringing.

'It's a long way to Tipperary,' countered the implacable Gloria, who hadn't.

It was the moment to strip off his shirt. She led him to the dais and expertly unfastened the buttons. 'Labour Reveals Treasure Chest', her press release had teased, with enough nudges and winks to ensure a full turn-out of local, national and international snappers.

'Arms wide, don't forget.'

How could he forget? Sprout, despite his position, was an intensely private man. He had always protected his body as fastidiously as a miser conceals his hoard. In his school sports days he had been the last to strip down for the communal bath,

Sunday

the first to wrap himself in a protective towel while everyone else strutted about in pimply glory. Until his recent ordeal, nobody but Edna, his wife, had seen his torso in decades. Was he really about to bare it to the whole world?

He was. Gloria stepped behind him to wrestle the shirt away, and he posed spreadeagled for the cameras under the unstinting sun with the party's aspirational credo emblazoned in deep red across his flabby pecs.

LABOUR'S
AGENDA

PUTTING FAMILIES FIRST
DRIVING EXTREME CONSUMPTION
ACCRUING BUDGET SURPLUSES
REWARDING INDUSTRIOUS SWEAT

The Number Three speech was mercifully short, consisting of strings of slogans occasionally interrupted by a reluctant verb. Sprout, although he found it difficult to project his voice while extending his arms, managed to work his way through a familiar litany of 'sweat-soaked workers', 'striving families' and 'deserving thrusters' until the cameras at last swivelled away and Gloria was satisfied.

'Hold your hand out, naughty boy,' she grinned, persisting with her music hall theme while easing him back into his shirt. 'How do you feel?'

But he could play that game, too.

'Like one of the ruins Cromwell knocked about a bit,' he said.

*

Lady Thatcher's Wink

'It seems to me, sire, that the nation is gagging for change.'

The king was trying as hard as he knew not to dislike Monty Muckle, not to feel that his blessed rural retreat was being violated. The weedless gravel paths struck out before them, now alongside borders burgeoning with fresh spring growth, now beneath shade-giving trees of exotic origin, but it was impossible to feel his customary contentment while the fellow was braying heavily in his ear. That 'sire' was not only mock medieval but delivered in the self-gratifying tone of fruity, world-wise condescension with which the man no doubt addressed the bartender of his local hostelry as 'squire'. He would certainly refer to it as a hostelry.

'Nobody knows you're here?' the edgy monarch asked for the second time in a minute. He felt frazzled. He had spent four hours circling his local airfield the previous evening, the pilot at last, with the fuel gauge on zero, obliged to land in a bumpy field full of cows.

'Not a soul,' Muckle replied for the second time.

'Because . . .'

'That's quite understood, sire. Our little secret.'

Quite what either of them expected it was impossible to be sure. If the latest polls were to be believed, Excalibur was rampant. Its manifesto spoke adoringly of the monarchy, but its fierce Englishness undoubtedly posed something of a difficulty.

'I do, you know,' the king said, 'have close links north of the border. Homes. Estates. Friendly keepers in kilts. Salt of the earth beaters.'

'Oh, don't you worry your head about that, sire. Believe me, I've tickled many a trout in Highland streams myself, and there's nothing I enjoy more than quaffing a Glenmorangie while sitting by a roaring peat fire with views of a loch.'

'And I was once Prince of Wales.'

'A remarkable principality, as I think we're supposed to call

Sunday

it. A fine people, no doubt. I've no problem with them at all.'

'As for the Irish, although I have my doubts about them, they can be pretty stroppy, you know. Not wise to cross them, in my considered opinion.'

'Don't I know it, sire? Haven't I had more than a few bouts of disagreement with the blarney boys over the years? I always found a mixture of tact and brute force did the trick. One night, during my more reprehensible young days, you might say, I took on three of them at a time outside the Hackney Empire, big brawny chancers fired up for a bit of . . .'

But they had reached a meeting of the ways, and the king impatiently waved him down.

'In short,' he said, 'none of that divisive business, Muckle. It's not the sort of thing we stand for. Quite out of the question.'

'Totally understood, sire. Totally.' Muckle found himself unusually pulled up in his verbal tracks, but only briefly. 'Try looking at our campaign as a marketing exercise. We need the English votes – haven't got much chance elsewhere, if I'm honest – and our USP is hating the rest of them. It goes down very well, but of course we don't mean any of it. Just a line we take, you understand. Politics.'

The monarch pointed to a gate set into a copper beech hedge.

'Where you came in,' he said.

'We haven't met,' Muckle grinned, respectfully taking his hand and retreating along the path with cheery insouciance.

A fresh peace descended on the hallowed acres in an instant. Birds sang again. The air became balmy. The old house, as he stepped inside, was pleased to see him.

'Do we have decorators in, Pimpkin?' he asked his secretary, who bowed his head in reverent greeting.

'Your majesty?'

'I thought I saw a fellow with a step-ladder.'

'Oh, that's the smallest photographer on Fleet Street, sir. You have an interview with the *Excess*.'

*

'Surprised to see you here, Turtle. In the circumstances, I mean.'

Sir Hilary Miles-Trumpington, all silver hair and sinuous elegance, looked him up and down suspiciously, taking in the laptop clamped under one arm and various smaller electronic devices sprouting from every pocket.

'I trust you're not going to use those things in the pavilion. It's a hangable offence.'

'As if I didn't know better, Trumps. But I daresay I shall have to do a little networking on the terrace.'

'Out of my earshot, I hope. Damn rocky start for the bankers. Three wickets down with just thirty on the board.'

'Game little buggers, aren't they?'

'Hunger's a great motivator, Turtle. I thought they were supposed to be plagued with rickets, but they seem pretty sturdy to me.'

'Leftist propaganda. Anyway, it's their scabby brats who go down with it. This lot have built their muscles on hand-outs.'

There were catcalls among the applause as another batsman succumbed and began the long trudge to the Lord's dressing room. The inaugural Bankers v Paupers match, some bright spark's modern take on the Gentlemen v Players encounters of yesteryear, wasn't going to plan.

'Thirty-two for four,' reported Turtle, who, albeit operating well beneath the MCC radar, *was* that bright spark. 'I hope we're going to get our money's worth.'

It was a colourful scene, as befitted a one-day match, the fielders kitted out in vivid orange and green to confirm their benefit claimant status, the batsmen (whose number six was at

Sunday

this moment asking the umpire to give him midde-and-leg) in rich Tory blue. Of course there had been the usual quibbles about bad taste, but nobody had been press-ganged. Indeed, a generous feature of the fixture was an agreement that, win or lose, the bankers would have a whip-round at the end of the match and share the bounty among their needy opponents, thereby embracing the government's much vaunted and commendably Christian 'Upper Crust' initiative which urged the better off to toss a little of their largesse at the feet of the poor. The charitable impulse added a gloss of sanctity, the chancellor of the exchequer had recently mused at a Guildhall dinner, to the sublime efficacy of his economic masterplan.

'That's making a funny kind of sound,' Sir Hilary said, pointing with subtle disdain.

'The glorious one!' Turtle chimed chummily, striding out to the terrace. 'I'm at the cricket, since you ask, but always open to your special kind of abuse. What about you?'

'Tower Hamlets. God's own country, though unfortunately he seems to have forsaken it. I thought you'd have rung to congratulate me by now.'

'Do tell me about this remarkable achievement, Gloria. The Sprout has finally stopped fluffing his lines, perhaps.'

'Our treasure chest, Gerry?'

'Ah, flabby flesh for a fairer Britain.'

'Not very good.'

'Agreed. I've been working on it, but the websters have got in first. The *Maul Online* has "Labour's campaign goes tits up." Is that any better?'

'Not much. We can take the ridicule. You know that's not the point.'

'Which is?'

'That we'll get splash coverage on the box tonight and in

tomorrow's papers. Unless you've something sensational up your sleeve.'

'Ah, that's why you called!'

'Not at all. Just craving a bit of praise where it's due.'

'A rare sign of weakness, Gloria.'

'Oh, come on – just this once!'

He laughed.

'Remarkable,' he conceded. 'But remarkably stupid.'

A few calls and messages later he found himself sitting next to a funereal looking man wearing a ghastly mistake of a tie.

'Greg Gripp,' he said, extending his hand. He swivelled in his seat. 'This is my guest, Ellie Stammers. A friend.'

'Oh, Mr Gripp,' she said, blushing. 'How nicely put!'

As they returned their gaze to the field, the batsman offered a thin edge to a fast delivery and the wicket keeper collapsed in an ugly heap after vainly trying to catch it. The umpire signalled a four.

'One of ours,' Gripp said.

'Ours?'

'Mine, I mean. I'm a handouts assessor. The keeper is on our books. Charlie Flout. Tendonitis, arrhythmia, pulmonary hypertension. He's marginal benefits, isn't he, Ellie?'

'Due for reappraisal in the morning, Mr Gripp.'

'Not a fast mover, but he used to play a bit and he still has the instinct. We thought we should come along to give him moral support.'

The next ball shaved the bails and eluded Flout's flapping gloves.

'He missed it again,' Turtle observed flatly.

'I blame the bowler,' Gripp said. 'Look at that pace. He'd never have got through on my watch.'

Sunday

The bankers, having staged something of a recovery, were all out for two hundred, at a convenient moment for the tea break. Turtle found himself a quiet corner and took a deep breath.

'Stu!' he launched himself warmly. 'Is this a good time?'

'Dreadful,' said Warbytton. 'But I've finished blathering for the day, if that's what you mean.'

'Barking.'

'Thank you.'

'I mean that's where you've been. We have it all monitored, Stu.'

'That doesn't surprise me in the least. And thanks for the geography lesson – these godawful places all look the same to me. What can I do for you?'

Turtle watched the groundsman running a light roller over the pitch. He waited for it to reach the end and turn.

'Just a word about style, Stu. A small word.'

'I don't do style, Turtle.'

'I think that's what I mean.' He paused again. The bankers were already out in the field, stretching and bending. 'We're holding up reasonably well in the polls, but the word is that we lack passion.'

'Reasonably well?'

'To be honest, Stu, there's a terrible scrabble for votes. That's what could turn it – passion.'

'Would you like to expatiate?'

'Sounding as if you meant it. As if you cared. How do I put this? The word is that you seem to be reading from a script.'

'Of course I am, Turtle. It's your wretched script, after all. Powerpoint and all that. You seemed pretty pleased with it, as I recall. Toe-curlingly so. I've memorised yards of it.'

'But you remember the prompts, Stu. The moments you wave your arms or pause for theatrical effect or raise your voice in justifiable anger. Grace notes.'

Lady Thatcher's Wink

'I'm not a blasted marionette, man.'

'You know the word I'm after . . .'

'Passion, as I recall.'

'The *semblance* of passion, Stu. That's enough. They need to feel that it's coming from the heart. That you engage.'

Now the openers were approaching the wicket, waving their bats to a heavy clattering of applause.

'Where the hell are you?' Warbytton asked.

'Oh, good shot!' Gripp enthused as Charlie Flout cut another seamer to the boundary with practised ease. It brought up his half-century.

'Should we make a note of this, do you think?' asked the dutiful Ellie. 'In view of tomorrow.'

'Only if he runs,' Gripp reassured her. 'They've all been fours and sixes so far, but he's done for if he gets from one end to the other.'

'I'll keep an eye,' she promised.

As the sun began to wester, the fielders cast shadows like hapless shades on the hallowed turf. The paupers, with two wickets in hand, needed only twenty to win.

'Good shot!' Gripp exclaimed again, allowing an arm to snake round Ellie's complaisant shoulders.

Gerry Turtle, passing behind them, experienced a rare moment of relaxation. This, after all, was a contest whose result really didn't matter to him at all, one which had no power to smash his reputation into little pieces.

*

At three minutes past nine, as the *Guinness Book of Records* would later carefully document, three passenger airliners sporting Argentine, Japanese and Uzbekistan liveries landed

Sunday

in close formation on a single runway at Heathrow, their wings clashing gently as they jostled for position on the tarmac and bordering grass.

One of the pilots had a heart attack, another announced his immediate retirement and the third stormed into the control tower, where he inflicted grievous wounds upon Power4Us operatives who, the company insisted, were doing their manful, nay heroic, best while awaiting enrolment on a training course.

It was an aviation first.

*

'You got fleas or something?' Edna Sprout asked as the marital bed shook and shivered beneath her. 'Or have we perhaps put out to sea?'

'Aaaargh!' moaned her husband, who was manically rubbing his chest with the flat of a hand, now here, now there, now everywhere. The second hand came up to join in.

'Some of us are trying to sleep,' she added, although there were only two of them on board, and that was one too many.

'Can't help it,' he gasped. 'Sorry. On fire. Help!'

It had been the longest day of his life, and far and away the most humiliating. His decorated thorax had been exposed to the gawp of a dozen London boroughs, to the ribaldry of countless profane wits and to the slow, steady basting of a relentless sun. Now it burned, tingled, itched, crawled.

'Didn't I warn you?,' said Edna, who thought that perhaps she had, and who certainly wasn't going to pass up the chance of a small victory. 'That Gloria Brightbloom.'

'A curse on her!' Sprout growled in agreement, rebelling for the very first time, and far too late. 'Help!'

Reluctantly opening her eyes, his loyal wife fished about in her bedside drawer and silently handed him not, as he rather

Lady Thatcher's Wink

expected in his delirium, a tube of soothing balm, but a sturdy crochet hook.

Equally silently he took it in his feverish fingers and began to scratch, now here, now there, now everywhere. Oh, the agony and the ecstacy!

*

For Sir Hilary it had been the perfect day, cricket at Lord's followed by supper at his club, but within the few steps from the cab to his front door and the similarly short interval during which Big Ben chimed twelve, he became the latest victim of the masked unicycle gangs, *aka* unicrims.

'Oh no you don't!' he cried, waving his cane at them.

But they did, as usual. Their deft spinning and weaving was a match for the fittest victim. There were four of them, buzzing about him like wasps at a jam jar, prodding, shoving, totally disorientating him until he collapsed between their wheels.

Knives were their favourite weapon, and a nasty looking blade was now held a few inches from his starched collar.

'Hand over, grandad,' said their leader in cheery tones.

What could he do but part with his wallet, two rings and (they had to rifle his pockets for it) a tab of cocaine?

'You're a disgrace,' he had the spirit to hiss as they prepared to wheel away. 'If you dared show your faces at my country estate we'd hunt you down like vermin.'

At which, of course, they laughed.

'You rural toffs won't ever understand our city way of life, mate,' one of them called over his shoulder. 'It's nature red in tooth and claw here.'

MONDAY

It had been a night even worse than the previous one for poor Warbytton. To the discomfort of suffocating heat was added the wild churning of unfathomable dreams. No sooner had he sunk into sleep than he felt himself assaulted by a braying din, first at an insistently high pitch, next wailing like a siren. Then, as he descended more deeply into his slumbers, he found himself following a distant light in a strange landscape inhabited by forms he was unable to recognise, not-quite-humans who reached out their hands to him and then withdrew the moment he approached. The more he chased after them, the more reluctant they were to meet him and the more exhausted he became in fruitless pursuit.

When the noise returned, a painful trilling, it took him an age to realise that it was his alarm clock. A quarter to six. Silencing it with a punch of his closed fist, he lay for a while in the netherworld of his dreams, a little smile at last on his lips. That guiding light among the murk, after all, needed no interpretation.

'A2,' he murmured contentedly.

This time he took a quick shower and dressed a little more formally before descending the stairs to what for him was now the Thatcher Room. It was a shock, on opening the door, to find that the figure energetically swabbing a window-pane was not the delicate sylph he sought but a fair-haired young man whose free arm was splinted and trussed up in a sling. He swung round to reveal a face heavily patched with plasters.

'I was looking for Anthropology Two,' Warbytton said.

'Plain old Applied Mathematics, I'm afraid,' the afflicted youth apologised, limping closer. 'Working towards a further

Lady Thatcher's Wink

degree in applied elbow grease. You'll find her upstairs. Second door on your right. A friend of yours?'

'Sort of.'

He retraced his steps and found her bringing shine to a mahogany table top.

'A2,' he murmured again. No, he hadn't imagined her loveliness.

'Warbie! I thought I'd scared you off. Too much reality.'

'I'm a bit braver than that, you know.'

The strangest thing was that when she had first begun to describe to him the lives of the lower orders, so very different from his own, he had imagined them to be as remote and beyond understanding as the South Sea Islanders she had for some reason omitted to study, but the more she spoke of what they thought and felt, the more like himself and the people he knew they seemed to be. This was obviously an outrageous idea, but it had preyed on his mind – and inhabited his dreams.

'I read one of your speeches in the papers yesterday,' she said, still rubbing away. 'To be honest, I was only checking that you really were the prime minister, because politics isn't really my kind of thing. Do you believe all that stuff about young people?'

'Possibly, I suppose. Possibly not. There's yards of it. What stuff?'

'Youth on the march to a better future. A nation only as vibrant as its young. The generations linking arms. I mean that kind of crap, Warbie.'

'It's aspirational,' he said, remembering his tutorials with Turtle. 'And we've statistics.' He closed his eyes in order to concentrate. 'A two per cent rise in apprenticeships over the last five years, rises in tuition fees pegged to ten per cent . . . '

He was unable to retrieve any more, and when he opened his eyes he saw her sitting down with a creamed cloth held

Monday

towards him, for all the world like a sword on which he was invited to fall.

'Fancy taking a turn?' she asked.

Warbytton, bridling, was tempted to point out who he was, but it seemed an inappropriately pompous things to do and, besides, she had already done her homework. He ignored the cloth.

'On an Up Yours agreement, of course.'

'Up Yours?'

'That's what we call your Unpaid Youth Recruitment Scheme. Thirty hours a week compulsory work experience in industry. After six months the lucky ones are promoted to Screw You.'

'Do tell me.'

'Short-term Contract Reward for Young Strivers. Three months without wages, but with travel costs paid.'

'And then?'

'The Finger. Final Government Employment Relief. A month at benefits level and then out on your ear if you can't land a permanent job.'

'Well, I never,' he said. 'We do seem to be doing rather a lot, don't we? I must ask Turtle about this. Do we treat you well here at Downing Street?'

'You don't employ me, Warbie. It's Power4Us. They employ just about everyone.'

'Ah yes, a Very Efficient Company,' he remembered from the screen. The Best in Outsourcing. Government at One Remove.'

'Who pay the lowest rates they can get away with.'

'But that's what we mean by efficiency, isn't it?' Warbytton said. He had never thought much about these matters before, and his head hurt when he did. 'You can't go splashing money about.'

Lady Thatcher's Wink

'How much do your cleaners get at Eggerton Hall?' she asked. 'Or don't you bother your head with any of that?'

'Not my bailiwick,' he readily conceded. 'I leave that to Jessie, who's a stickler for every last tedious detail concerning the servants. I mean the staff. Highly Valued Staff. But I'm sure it's the living wage.'

She gurgled.

'Well, I suppose we are all *alive*,' she said.

An unaccustomed silence fell between them. It was broken by the opening of a door and the abrupt entrance of a veritable adonis. He was tall and somewhat burly, with a shock of gingerish hair, he had a raffish glint in his eye and he wore, with dashing self-confidence, a monogrammed dressing gown over scarlet silk pyjamas.

'Ooooh,' she whispered, despite herself.

'Freddie!' exclaimed Warbytton. 'What the hell are you doing here?'

'Don't sound so surprised, pate,' Freddie replied. 'Didn't mummy tell you I was coming?'

'She did threaten it. When did you arrive?'

'Early hours. Had a bit of trouble, to tell the truth. The GPS brought me to the end of Downing Street, where I found a set of gates which the men in blue refused to open for me. I tossed them the keys and told them to park it, but they came over all arsey. Who pays their wages, I'd like to know. In fact that's what I did ask them in plain man's language.'

'Oh God,' Warbytton said.

'They wouldn't even let *me* through, let alone the waggon, but I did a bit of nimble footwork to avoid the scrum and I was touching down outside while the Keystone Cops were still distantly panting in pursuit. Acutely comical!'

'You didn't . . .'

'So then I hopped over some low railings to force a window,

Monday

which set the bells of hell ringing, and I'd hardly got my legs over the sill before the flashing blue lights were playing *son et lumière* all over the facade. A poetic sight, pate, I'm sure you'd have agreed had you been awake to see it.'

'Bullingdon,' was all Warbytton found it possible to say.

'Fortunately one of the senior rozzers recognised me – some minor fracas from days gone by – and we were able to sort things out without too much difficulty and expense.'

It was only at this moment that he caught sight of the pretty girl with the cleaning cloth.

'Well, well,' he said, stepping forward. 'Oh, my!' He crooked a forefinger under her chin to tilt her face towards his. 'Who do we have here then?'

'Anthropology Two,' Warbytton replied weakly. He suddenly seemed far removed from the tender scene playing out before him. He might not have been in the room at all.

She gazed up at her lusty assailant, her eyes glistening, her cheeks flushed.

'Hello,' she said. 'I'm Chloe.'

*

The shopping mall at Brent Cross, with a nominal aptness that passed him by, turned out to be Sprout's golgotha. Stripped for the Number Six, extreme consumption, speech ('Let virtuous greed be the engine to defeat vicious poverty'), he spread his arms before a phalanx of designer bags and immediately saw the Brightbloom visage darken.

'Cover up!' she called in horror from behind the crowd.

What could she mean? For the very first time he felt glad to have his shirt off, free from the irritation of cotton on harrowed flesh. He stretched even more vigorously than usual, while the cameras flashed and, he couldn't help but notice, his audience

Lady Thatcher's Wink

laughed and applauded in a manner somewhat less than respectful.

'Many a true word, Sprouty!' someone piped up insolently.

'Shirt!' the desperate Gloria burbled, still only half way towards him.

To one side of him there was a mirrored pillar. Turning to it, he beheld the cruel effect of the sun in blistering his innocent skin and of Brenda's crochet hook in raising angry welts upon it. Most of the lettering had faded to an angry blur, leaving only fragments of words around the centre of his chest and reducing LABOUR'S AGENDA to the grim sounding OUR END.

And what was their destiny to be? His eyes drifted lower, and he trembled to read the prediction:

LIES

CONS

RUIN

DUST

'Let's all go down the Strand,' Gloria grimaced with as much humour as she could manage. She seized a campaign banner, draped it over his head and hurried him away, for all the world like a suspected child molester escorted into a police van. 'Or at least out of here as quickly as we can.'

'Laugh and grow fat like me,' was all he could muster in reply.

*

'We don't normally allow conjugal visits, Mrs Flout,' Gripp told her. 'Although, in the circumstances . . .'

'Thrown out of our home,' she sobbed, dabbing at her eyes with a crumpled tissue.

Monday

'I mean in view of Charlie's triumph,' Gripp explained. 'Housing is another department altogether.'

'But you can understand Mandy's feelings,' Charlie said. 'We've been there for thirty years, and now they're throwing us out. To Milton Keynes.'

'Many fine roundabouts in Milton Keynes,' Gripp offered.

'Away from all our family and friends,' Mrs Flout said, 'because they want to pull down our flats and put up posh apartments for bankers.'

Gripp shook his head.

'This isn't my area of expertise, but don't you think bankers need homes, too? And they wouldn't feel comfortable in a common or garden chicken coop of a flat, would they?'

'Sounds reasonable when you put it like that,' Charlie said, 'but they don't have to get by on handouts.'

Now Gripp sprang to life.

'Thank you for reminding me, Charlie,' he smiled. 'Ellie, let's have the dossier, please.'

She opened it on the desk before him.

'As you've probably guessed,' Gripp said, 'we're going to have to stop these payments. You weren't entirely straight with me, were you?'

'Wasn't I?'

'Ellie and I came to watch you at Lord's yesterday. A very fine outing it was. May I remind you of that winning run? How you streaked down the wicket?'

'It was the very last ball,' Flout protested. 'I had to try it. And I collapsed before I got to the other end.'

'But you crossed with the other batsman, Charlie. You must have run all of twelve yards with a bat in your hand. That's about eleven metres in new money. I've watched the replays several times.'

'Please, Mr Gripp,' Mandy said. 'He's not the man he was.'

'We must all strive to be best men we can be,' Gripp said, 'or woman in your particular case, and I couldn't look at myself in the mirror if I failed in my duty to society. It's almost a religion with me, Mrs Flout.'

'So what can we do?' Charlie asked, breathing less freely than when he came in.

'Try again in Milton Keynes,' advised Gripp. 'You may find someone whose morals are more questionable than mine.'

*

Warbytton caught Lambert Probus, the chancellor of the exchequer, as they left a crisis campaign meeting. The word 'passion' still rang in his ears with the sonority of the Lutine bell marking the loss of a ship at sea.

'A couple of minutes, Bertie, if you can spare them,' he said. 'I'm a little perplexed about money matters.'

'Aren't we all, Sturge? We have to pretend not to be. How can I help?'

'It's the rather hefty divide between the people at the top and those at the bottom. I'd like to be able to give a sensible answer to that.'

'Got a difficult constituent, have you? It's hard to fob them off sometimes.'

'She is pretty unshakeable. The pay gap and all that.'

'The first thing to note, Sturge, is that we don't say "pay gap" any more. That's a bit charged, don't you think? I mean, with a bit of imagination you can almost see the thing. We changed that some while ago to "achievement differentials", until people began to realise it meant the same thing. Now we say "accruement variables". I'll let you know when it becomes something else.'

'But high pay, low taxes . . .'

Monday

'Right, a quick lesson, Sturge. Just put yourself in the position of a director on the board of some financial institution who has the fate of all sorts of investors in his hands. In fact he's probably on several boards at once, so you can imagine that he's a vital cog in the national economy.'

'Although he doesn't make anything.'

'He makes profits, Sturge, don't you see. And now imagine that we came along and said we were going to put a cap on his pay and bonuses or increase his taxes. What would he do then?'

'Work a bit harder so that he could keep up his standard of living?'

Probus laughed.

'The very opposite. It's human nature. Incentives! If we make life harder for him he'll simply not think it worth his while to sweat on the company's behalf. He may even catch the next flight out to New York or Hong Kong. That's why we've put everyone on a single band of tax.'

'I see. And those at the bottom? The workers rather than the shirkers, I mean. Don't they want more money, too?'

'Of course they do, but that would be a disaster. Just put yourself in the position of someone who stacks shelves or fusses over old people in a care home. What would happen if you gave her a pay rise or cut her taxes?'

'She'd be inspired to work even harder?'

'Come, come Sturge. It's human nature. All she really wants to do is sit on the sofa watching TV while nibbling something horribly fattening. Incentives! Give her too much and she'll decide she doesn't need to lift a finger. Keep her pay low and she has to sweat all hours to get what she needs. The precious dignity of labour! That's how the economy thrives.'

'So everyone's happy.'

'The people who matter are happy.'

Lady Thatcher's Wink

*

'I'm sorry, Emre, but I've an appointment this evening.'

Taz had settled his rump on a roll of Turkish carpet to take the call. Was it only one o'clock? The working week had already lasted far too long.

'Appointment?'

'I'm being taken around 10 Downing Street. A private showing. I couldn't really say no to that, could I?'

He needed a few seconds to take it in.

'Where I've been working, remember,' she added. 'The prime minister's pad.'

He sounded suitably nonplussed.

'Are you telling me Warbytton has actually offered to give you the tourist treatment?'

'Not Warbytton, no. Well yes, I suppose Warbytton.'

'Is he in disguise or something?'

'I mean that it's his son.'

'Oh.'

She could tell from the crackle in her ears that he had moved, and seconds later she heard the clatter of a keyboard. It was Taz's boast never to be more than twenty paces from an IT terminal.

'So this is . . .'

'Freddie,' she said.

'Frisky Freddie, the fillies' favourite.'

'Really?'

'Came bounding from court, having survived his third paternity suit in two years.'

'Oh.'

'With a pretty girl on either arm. Or' (there was a little more tapping) 'I can offer you Further disgrace for Warbytton heir.

Monday

Young Freddie, bailed after a fracas at the Kaffir Club, arrived in court riding a bull African elephant which doused the magistrates with water, left a steaming mess on the courtroom floor and had to be downed with shots from a tranquilising gun. The case was adjourned pending psychiatric reports.'

'I'm enjoying this,' said Chloe, as engagingly honest as she was alluring.

'And then you've a choice between PM's son in new race slur, Freddie W. goofs again and The curse of the Warbyttons. When are you seeing him?'

'At six.'

'And then?'

'He's promised to show me a few places he knows.'

'So it's a date.'

'An appointment.'

'It's a date, Chloe.'

'Goodbye, Emre.'

He returned to the roll of carpet and sat staring into space for a while. He had his new material.

*

Dalton Frisby, for twenty years editor of the *Daily Maul*, was used to picking winners, and it was obvious to his chief leader writer that the present political maelstrom had unnerved him.

'When it comes to it we'll have to back someone, Snitchy, but they're all pathetic gobshites.'

'Totally agreed,' replied Arnold Snitch, his thin smile apparently a dutiful assent to Frisby's unspoken belief that the five-times newsman of the year could run the country better than any of the sorry contenders currently parading their inadequacies before the public, but actually a rueful acceptance that he would all too soon be harnessing Miltonian eloquence

Lady Thatcher's Wink

in portraying one of them as a born leader, an adroit statesman in a world of dangerous foreign jackasses, a friend to the justly rich and a reluctant protector of the striving poor.

'What's your gut feeling, Snitchy?'

'Same as yours. God rot 'em all. We obviously won't be backing Labour. Warbytton lacks grip. Excalibur are in good heart, but the *Excess* are bound to endorse them. Not good company to be in.'

'We could argue for a coalition of all the talents, which is probably what it will come down to anyway – minus the talent, naturally. The mangey Tory fox alongside a couple of tame rabbits.'

'I could make a case for the Anti-tax Alliance, I suppose. An outsourced government, with any regrettably necessary income raised by swingeing fines imposed for wrongful behaviour, whatever that might turn out to be. Quixotic, but they're in line for a few seats.'

'And what about the Pink Party? We always support the little woman in the *Maul*, don't we? Bless her cotton knickers.'

'As long as she knows where she stands, Dalt.'

'Or lies, I think you mean. But they're not asking for too much. Nothing that can't be forgotten after the event. Cheaper cosmetics and that sort of thing. Do you remember equal pay, maternity benefits, supported child care, places on the board and all that chilling nonsense? We ridiculed feminism to death years ago, thank God.'

'I'll work up a few scenarios, shall I? We've got twenty-four hours before we need to decide.' He smiled as thinly as before. 'Time for a dynamic leader to emerge.'

'Ha bloody ha!'

There was a knock on the door, which was respectfully edged open. A pair of spectacles appeared in the gap, with a neat beard and a bright yellow bowtie beneath it. Even a complete outsider would have known that this was the art director. A pair of brown corduroys dutifully joined the ensemble.

'Ready for us?'

'Let's roll, Fergie!'

He swivelled in his chair with a familiar feeling of deep satisfaction as the paper's editorial team filed into the room for the afternoon conference, each of them palpably fired up, on edge and eager to please. Frisby had the reputation of a man modest in his habits and socially reclusive, but the pallidity of his private life was more than compensated by the godlike power he exercised over his trained communicators and, through them, the public at large. He daily set the national agenda, instructing his readership what to hate, what to fear and sometimes (a rare concession) what to admire.

'The immigrants, Harry,' he prompted the news editor. 'Persuade me.'

It was pure theatre. Here he reclined with the submissions list in his hand, and there they perched awkwardly on their chairs, sleeves rolled, plastic coffee cups gripped in tense fingers, competing for column inches and the moment's glory.

'We've stood this one up,' the ruddy faced Harry Scutt assured him. 'Laughter's been heard from inside the Stepney bongo bin. Three witnesses have confirmed it, two of them happy to be named.'

'So this is Laughing at Our Generosity?'

'I think it's more They Party While We Pay, Dalt. There's been some kind of entertainment in there, and I don't just mean improvised drum kits from broom handles and upturned packing cases. We think one of the staff has taken games inside.'

'Doesn't sound like Power4Us. They're trained to be brutal.'

'There's always one bad apple. We've even heard rumours of English lessons, although they were outlawed last year.'

Lady Thatcher's Wink

'Teaching Them How to Claim Our Jobs. But I prefer the laughter story. That's a real slap in the face. Yes, Fergie?'

'We've a cartoon already roughed out for it,' the art director offered. He stood up and brought it forward. 'Happy natives chanting around a pot with a John Bull figure being boiled alive in it. Not sure what the message on the hatband's going to be. Something like Generous to a Fault, I suppose.'

Frisby frowned.

'But they're not all black in there, are they?'

'Not all "black" black, if that's what you mean. Quite a few eastern Europeans. Lots of Uzbeks.'

'This might seem a tad racist to the bleeding heart brigade, Fergie. We need a couple of paler faces and some kind of quaint generic entertainment. Can we have a zither?'

'But then we couldn't very well include a missionary pot.'

The news editor came to the rescue.

'Forget the pot. How about we have these assorted drunken ravers dancing on the sands of a desert island while John Bull is offshore in a tiny boat and sinking under the waves.'

'Not bad, Harry,' Frisby conceded. 'The hatband could read something like Swamped by a Rising Tide. Have your man work on it, Fergie. Now what about a front page image, Bob?'

The picture editor handed over a clutch of proofs.

'Has to be Sprout's epitaph, I suppose,' he said.

Frisby shook his head.

'It'll have whiskers by the morning – been all over the internet for hours already. We'll put it on the op ed with Frank's Labour Fading Fast piece. Who's the dolly with the sharply exposed knockers?'

'Valmai Partridge, the Pink Party leader. Not a new pic, as you can probably guess, but nobody else has got it. Turns out she used to be an escort.'

'A tart,' Frisby said. 'Good to wake up to, don't you think?

Monday

I'd like to splash that. We might take the Background of Shame shock-horror line. Vampish Valmai in the Pink. Vile example to young girls and all that.'

'Except, remember,' Snitch broke in, 'that we may possibly write her up as a potential coalition partner on Wednesday.'

'Okay, so we lay off the moral line, but let's have her.'

'While we're on politicos,' the news editor came back, 'don't forget Warbytton's son breaking into Number Ten last night. We've some juicy quotes from one of the constables on duty, plus you should have some of the snaps he took, Bob.'

'Didn't bring them,' the picture editor said guardedly. 'Poor quality. The only good one shows the little bastard's gleaming arse as he attempts to climb through a window. Wouldn't inflict that on anyone.'

'We're not running the story,' Frisby said, to a rare silence.

'Not at all?'

'Not at all, Harry. Bad timing. I've had a word with Gerry Turtle and we've come to an agreement. Next, please!'

A bronzed young man raised his hand.

'I forget who you are,' said Frisby, who liked to squash at least one member of his staff at each meeting.

'Luke Freemantle,' he replied, visibly abashed. 'Your new sports editor.'

'I thought it had to be something like that,' Frisby said. He regarded the back pages as akin to something unpleasant permanently stuck to the soles of his shoes. 'Unicycles.'

'A good anti-Europe yarn,' Freemantle enthused, eagerly picking up the cue. 'There's a decision today on Britain's bid to have unicycling included as an event in the Java Olympics. Most of our European friends are voting against.'

'Friends?'

'Rivals . . . Enemies . . . Traitors . . . Anyway, they know we're the only country who stand a chance of gold, thanks to our millions of practitioners. We can stir up a good deal of bile about that. It's an absolute gift.'

'Unbalanced. Make sure you throw that in.' He consulted his sheet. 'Unbalanced is good. And what's this about the Bankers v Paupers match? That was this morning's news, Mr Freemantle.'

'Luke.'

'We have to earn our pleasantries here, young man. And we have to display a nose for news.'

'It's a development, Dalt . . . Mr Frisby . . . Sir . . . The hero of the hour.'

Frisby rose in his chair, open-mouthed with rage.

'I mean Charlie Flout. He won it for the Paupers with the last ball of the innings, and this morning he lost his benefits for being too fit.'

'Still old news, matey,' the news editor broke in, seizing the chance to curry favour with his boss. 'We've run that on the website since midday. Lord's Star Batsman in Fake Disability Disgrace. Worth a few pars in the morning, I agree, but we run two or three stories like that every day.'

Freemantle took a deep breath, uncertain what tone to take.

'It's worse,' he said at last. 'He and his wife were evicted from their flat today. They couldn't take any more. They climbed the stairs to the roof, tied themselves together with their orange bibs and jumped, flattening an unfortunate unicyclist in the process. The inquests open on Friday.'

A sombre mood settled on the room for a few inconvenient seconds.

'So, Harry, is it Fake Disability Batsman in Suicide Pact?' Frisby wondered aloud, 'or Lords Disability Cheat Does Decent Thing?'

'I'd like to know about the cyclist,' the news editor replied. 'Was he a bib wearer?'

'Not as far as I know,' Freemantle said. 'Recreational.'

'Then perhaps Innocent Rider Killed by Abject Suicide Pair.'

'I'll leave you to work on it,' Frisby told him. 'Now we've just tomorrow's leader to consider.'

'It's about time we had one of our moral high-horse pieces,' Snitch suggested. 'An uplifting address to the po-faced, right-thinking reader. I always enjoy working myself up into a pious lather. How about an attack on cynicism in public life?'

'Go on.'

'You know, all that sneering at businessmen who only want the best for society. The distrust of government ministers who ditto. Envy of the rich, as if they haven't sweated for it. The *Maul* calls for a return of trust, deference and gratitude for the status quo.'

Frisby, beaming with pleasure, closed the meeting in his usual fashion, clapping his hands together and (all too briefly the Duke of Wellington in disguise) letting out a cry of 'Up boys and at 'em!' He watched them set off for the battlefield, a personal army slaying the enemies of sound British common sense, burnished tradition and hard-won privilege, bravely laying waste to foul cynicism.

*

'Fancy seeing you here, Anthropology Two!' Daphne exclaimed, carefully stacking tins of best value spam (the luridly coloured label said so) on a shelf already sagging with 3-for-2 carrots, easy-mash potato and 'Crafty Shopper' peas.

'I didn't know you worked in this place,' Chloe said. 'Don't you ever take a break?'

'Voluntary, love. People need a hand. Who's your interesting looking friend?'

They glanced across at the household goods aisle (recycled

Lady Thatcher's Wink

paper towels, bargain buy plastic cups, neat-fit nappies), where a man wearing a strangely assorted outfit of Australian bush hat with dangling corks, oversize sunglasses, gaudy hawaiian shirt, khaki shorts, knee-length sky-blue socks and open-toed sandals stood immobile in a seeming trance.

'Just a friend,' she said.

'Has he got a voucher?'

'No, I wanted to show him what a food bank's like. He's conducting some research – if you don't mind.'

'Oh, I don't mind, dear. Another one doing a degree, is he? Must be a one of those mature students. Never ceases to amaze me what you educated folk bother your huge brains with. Is he another anthropology?'

'Politics more like.'

'Then maybe he'll be my Politics Four one day. Would he like a sheet with the rules on it?'

'I'm sure that would be helpful.'

But before she could approach him the eccentric scholar had lumbered towards a weary looking woman in worn clothes. An elbow protruded from her cardigan and her toes were showing through cracks in her shoes.

'Salmon?' he asked, pointing at a packet in the cardboard box she clutched in her scrawny hands.

'Fish.'

'And this is pork?'

'Meat.'

'What about your third course?'

'I beg your pardon.' She turned to Daphne for protection. 'What's this weird bloke want?'

'Don't worry, Mrs Threadgold. He's from the university. Can't you tell from his bearing? Completely harmless, I'm sure. He'll probably be writing a prognosis about it.'

'Thesis,' Chloe glossed.

Monday

'I'm not used to having people prod about in my things. What else does he want to know?'

'What else do you want to know?' Daphne asked.

He inclined his head.

'This is tonight's supper for you and your husband, I imagine, with your tipple of choice to be sourced elsewhere?'

'Do me a favour, professor nosey-parker,' she exploded. 'First, the worthless bleeder you're referring to hasn't been seen for years. Second, if he values his health he'd better not think of showing his ugly, misshapen face here again. Third, this lot will last me and my four kids the best part of three days if I'm very careful. Now put that in your prologue and smoke it!'

Chloe gently tugged at his elbow.

'Time to be going, Warbie,' she whispered.

*

Monty Muckle breezed into his local betting shop after a happy day of pint quaffing and crowd pleasing.

'Evening, squire!' he greeted the grizzled teller at the only window still left open. 'What are your odds on Excalibur for a straight win?'

The reply took a time to come, and seemed to be addressed with patient deliberation to someone of limited intelligence.

'Would that be at Wetherby?'

'I mean the general election on Thursday.'

'Oh, that.'

'You have heard of it, I suppose? People go into booths and put a cross by a name.'

'Very droll.' He pointed languidly, affecting to be the most bored individual on the planet. 'There's a list on the wall if you can be bothered to look.'

Muckle inspected it.

'Ten to one. That's not very generous, is it? Has it moved today?'

'Hard to say,' the teller said. 'Wouldn't know.'

'It was twelve to one this morning ,' a helpful voice called out from somewhere behind the counter.'

'That's what I'd have expected,' Muckle said smugly. 'And what are the odds on Monty Muckle for prime minister?'

'Who?'

'Monty Muckle. He's the leader of Excalibur.'

His combatant ran a slow finger down a sheet of paper, apparently with no success.

'A Ronny Suckle,' he called behind him. 'We got odds on him? Heavily *against* him, I should reckon. Strange name.'

'Monty Muckle,' repeated Muckle with heavy emphasis.

'Once again?'

But the distant voice came to the rescue again: 'Twenty to one. Came back five today.'

'That's what I'd have expected,' Muckle said. 'Thanks.'

'You going to place a bet then?'

'Did it a month ago, pal,' he said jauntily, turning on his heel. 'I could spot the trend. That's how you beat the bookies.'

As he returned to the street the voice at the back of the shop said 'That was Monty Muckle himself.'

'Course it was.'

'You knew that all along?'

'Course I did. How could you mistake him? Fake tan, quiffed hair, cheesy grin. I may end up voting for him, but he's the sort of cocky bastard you just want to punch in the mouth.'

*

Here's hot breakin news, frenz, from de heart of what dey likes to style 'government' but what is – and doan we all

Monday

know it for a sorry, sleazy troot – a wicked scam spun aginst you, me and every other poor brother and sister locked outside their small and dirty clan.

Taz paused in his tetchy tirade to gaze once more upon the image so artfully touched up by Chloe's dextrous fingers. What energy there was in those threshing limbs, and with what salacious pleasure did Mrs Thatcher entice the viewer in to her bower of lustful desires! He uploaded it to his blog.

And when I says dirty, amigos, I beg you to commodate this fragment of porn straight from the walls of that politicos temple Number Ten Downing Street. *Thatcher image* This fierce chick, as some of youse may register, is Mrs Margaret Thatcher, a Tory icon they elevated to a grand dame in dayz gone by. Feck man, some horny drongo inside this holy of holies has made her the madame of a friggin knockin shop!!!

He took a deep breath, closed his eyes the better to remember the lines he had rehearsed a dozen times during the day, and hammered out his final paragraph.

Will they manage to finger this horny drongo? I ask youse whether they'll even dare. Here's a clue, frenz. Who should light up at his dad's pad the other night but Fast Freddie Warbytton aka Filthy Freddie aka The Curse of the Warbyttons aka Frisky Freddie the Fillies Favourite. Yes folks, the prime minister's randy son! He's top drawer – is he a top drawer, too?

He'd worked on it too long to know whether that was a good joke or an appalling one. It didn't matter. He took one more look at the picture, then hit the key for it to go forth and multiply.

*

Lady Thatcher's Wink

Midnight. The doorway sleepers all along the Strand stirred in their thin blankets and stroked their dogs to silence. Jesus, what kind of time was this for some mad Australian tourist to come waltzing along, eager for someone to talk to? And, even under the neon lights, wasn't it far too dark for sunglasses?

They felt like calling the police to take him away.

TUESDAY

Warbytton was poking a well buttered toast finger into the first of two glistening boiled eggs when his earnest young PPS interrupted the breakfast ritual.

'Sorry, sir, but there's been a bit of bother overnight.'

'Oh, lord!' He took a hearty bite and allowed himself a swig of strong black coffee. 'That blasted Freddie!'

'You've heard?'

'No, it's simply a logical assumption. What's he done this time?'

'His guilt isn't yet confirmed, sir. Would you like to follow me downstairs?'

Warbytton shook his head. At this moment it occurred to him that he hadn't shaken his head often enough over the past few months. He was, after all, and despite all, prime minister of one of the mightiest nations on earth – according to Turtle's Powerpoint, at least. Would Disraeli have been hurried from his breakfast table by an eager flunkey? What brave creature (he almost laughed aloud to imagine it) would have dared even float the idea before the appetitive Winston Churchill?

'After my second chuckie, Jonathan. It's not a matter of life and death, I presume?

'No, sir.'

Thus morally fortified, he followed the eggs with a slice of toast liberally spread with thick-rind marmalade and enjoyed a leisurely second cup of coffee before at last shaking the crumbs from his trousers and rising to accompany his restless adjutant.

'Thank you, sir.'

Their destination was the Thatcher room where, upon entering, Warbytton at once saw that the reconfigured portrait had been taken from the wall and, propped against a pile of books, was now prominently displayed on a table. The phrase Exhibit A came effortlessly to mind.

'Sweet Jesus!' he breathed, disingenuously and somewhat mechanically from constant practice.

'It's been ... interfered with,' Jonathan said. The seriousness of his steel-rimmed glasses was softened by the merest glint of amusement in his eyes. 'By an insider.'

'Dreadful!'

'And I'm afraid, sir, that it's all over the internet and has made the later editions of the nationals.' He crossed the room to a side table and came back clutching a heavy pile of the morning papers. 'It's nothing less than a scandal.'

Warbytton wished that the sentence had been spoken with less relish. He desperately wished himself, as so often during this wretched interregnum, back in the peaceful, hallowed acres of Eggerton Hall.

'The chief of staff and Mr Turtle are on their way.'

The newspapers were unfolded and flattened out on the table top, where they trumpeted their outrage. The portrait was on the front of every one of them.

DAME MAGGIE TRADUCED! lamented the *Excess*, so grievously overcome as to employ a verb few of its readers would confidently translate, let alone ever use.

> *A portrait of the former Conservative leader Margaret Thatcher, donated by a party supporter and hung inside 10 Downing Street, has been foully desecrated by a perverted graffiti artist to suggest she was part of an unspeakable orgy in the grounds of the Houses of Parliament.*
>
> *This disgraceful defacement, revealed by the controversial blogger Taz, horrified No 10 security guard Bruce Withers when this newspaper tipped him off about it last night.*
>
> *'I just shook,' he said. 'It was a truly disgusting sight.'*

Tuesday

The sensitive Withers appeared similarly shocked in every account. The seriousness of this 'vile crime against common decency' was, for the *Maul*, unarguably authenticated by the security man's macho credentials. Their scabrous penman Frank Bludgeon, his gloating Labour Fading Fast feature unceremoniously spiked, had been pulled the worse for wear from his favourite late-night drinking den to rustle up an instant 800-worder.

> *Here is a hero who saw jungle service with the SAS, who swam the English Channel in the depths of winter, who beat to a pulp three armed robbers at a high street bank and who safely piloted a Boeing 707 to an emergency landing at Heathrow after the crew collapsed from food poisoning. And yet, standing before this abomination, he admits to being stricken to his core.*
>
> *'It was,' he told us, 'like seeing your wife violated before your very eyes. These drawings depict unspeakable acts.'*
>
> *This has become a litmus test for a Tory party in disarray. Find and punish the culprit now, or pay the ultimate penalty at the ballot box.*

The *Blither*, free of any rightwing sympathies, highlighted a rumour only cautiously alluded to by its rivals.

FRIGHTFUL FREDDIE FINGERED FOR MAGGIE PORN

Self-styled street blogger Taz has accused the accident prone PM's son Freddie 'Fly-by-Night' Warbytton of perpetrating the sensational cartoon insult inflicted on former premier Margaret Thatcher.

No evidence is yet forthcoming, but the mucky scrawling of her portrait with scenes of sexy cavorting can only have been perpetrated by someone inside the securely guarded portals of 10 Downing Street.

'Where on earth are these fabled portals?' Warbytton mused aloud. 'And what,' he asked, 'has Freddie got to say?'

'Flew by night, sir. Done a runner.' Jonathan was evidently a keen reader of murder mysteries. 'His bed hasn't been slept in. That's bound to arouse suspicions.'

'Hardly, I think. He sleeps in other people's beds far more often than his own.'

Gerry Turtle and Fitzroy Julian arrived together, hands briefly raised in silent greeting, an air of serious business to be done. Turtle, who equally silently signalled coffee to the PPS with a tilting of a hand to his mouth, seemed diminished in the presence of the Downing Street chief of staff, a pale moon to his glowing sun. He liked to appear suave, but alongside the lordly Julian always felt merely sly.

'What a bugger,' he said, by way of an opener.

They approached the exhibit and examined it closely.

'Rather good,' Julian murmured. 'A definite improvement.'

'It alarmed the security man,' Warbytton said. 'Like seeing his wife being violated apparently.'

'Well, he can go home and do it himself now,' Turtle retorted. 'Out on his ear. Not that he'll give a monkey's with all the dirty money flowing into his bank account.' He turned to Julian. 'I've called in Power4Us for a dressing down. Will you do it or shall I?'

'My pleasure,' Julian smiled in anticipation. It was for just such an oil-on-troubled-waters moment as this that his years of subtle training in the civil service had prepared him. There was no point in the job unless there were monstrous cock-ups. 'Do you have a view, Warbs, about your son's likely involvement?'

'None at all. As far as I'm concerned it's all a lot of hot air.'

'Of course, of course. But now that there's a very large balloon floating above our heads we shall have to find a way of deflating it.'

Tuesday

'The semblance of a crisis *is* a crisis,' Turtle threw in. 'But don't worry, Stu – I'll work up a couple of lines for you to throw into today's speeches.'

'Really?' Warbytton said, in a tone Turtle didn't recognise.

*

It was the freedom of the airwaves for Freeman Goodblow. In his years as prime minister he had learned to curb his natural abrasiveness when jousting with the trenchant Jason Blurt on what the BBC liked to call its 'flagship' early morning radio programme. Now that the shackles were off he could gloriously indulge himself in filleting the party which had so abjectly hung him out to dry for a series of trivial offences.

'Can you really imagine this happening on my watch?' he demanded. 'Discipline's gone to pot.'

'You made a daily check of the pictures on the wall?' Blurt challenged him mischievously.

'Didn't need to, Jason. I ran a reign of terror in there, believe me. You have to boss Downing Street exactly as you boss the country. Stand by your beds! Deliver the goods or get out! The devil take the hindmost! Winner takes all! And do you think some Power4Us underling would have gone blabbing to the press like that wretched fellow who's all over the papers today? He'd have known what would happen to him.'

'Which is what, precisely?'

'What I did to those cats, ha ha!'

'You admit . . .'

'A joke, Jason, a joke. What I was *alleged* to have done to those cats. I've made my position on cats very clear.' (For a moment he was in Turtle mode.) 'As for the portrait, do you think any captain of industry would ever again be foolish enough to entrust such a gem to Downing Street?'

Lady Thatcher's Wink

'You're referring to . . .'

'To Bill Botting of Botting Armaments. He personally put the Thatcher portrait into my hands as a token of what he called our valued special relationship – his very words. This is a man who was prepared to donate several million pounds to the Tory cause, who bid a cool hundred thousand at one of our fund-raising dinners to play a round of bridge with the PM and two fruity dollies of his choice, who flew the flag for Britain whenever he shook hands on weapons deals for which we'd helped oil the wheels all around the world.'

'You mean Lord Botting of Botting?'

'As he is now, yes. Wonderful chap. Always stands his round. Occasionally visits the House . . .'

'So a cynic might suggest,' Blurt interrupted, at last finding his angle, 'that this Thatcher portrait played a part, however small, in buying Mr Botting's peerage.'

Goodblow allowed a small silence to separate them.

'Jason,' he resumed piously, 'I'm afraid the BBC once again shows itself immune to reality. As the Iron Lady herself might have said, money is like the black ball in snooker – only the Tory party and its friends know how to chalk the cue so that it always ends up in the right pockets.'

*

'Eggie, what is this nonsense? They can't possibly believe that Freddie perpetrated that drawing.'

Warbytton held the phone well away from his ear.

'Well he's not a stranger to foul-ups, Jessie. Or, if we're honest, to the occasional romp.'

'I'm not talking about rumpy-pumpy, Eggie, for goodness sake. Do you take me for a prude all of a sudden? Just think back to his schooldays. Do you remember his artwork?'

'Of course not.'

'Those heavy sheets of paper with daubs all over them he used to bring home and expect to be stuck to the walls? A house, path and garden? He couldn't even put the chimney on the roof. And the smoke blew in two directions at once. He couldn't draw a straight line if he had a ruler in his hand.'

'They say he's done a runner.'

'What kind of company are you keeping down there?'

'I mean he didn't come home last night.'

'Then you have to speak up for him, Eggie. Tell them it can't be him. I switched on the radio this morning and didn't hear a peep from you.'

'I try not to do radio. It finds you out.'

'Then I'll have to send Diana down. She's in an interestingly fragile state just now, and I'm sure she'd appreciate the change of scene.

He yelped.

'It's an ultimatum,' she said. 'Set the record straight or you get both Freddie *and* Diana.'

*

'He's still there, Mr Gripp,' Ellie said.

'Greg. Please.'

'Moving along the line. Taking notes now.'

'Call the police.' He passed her a sheet of paper with a name and telephone number on it. 'It's a public order offence at the very least.'

'But they all seem happy to talk to him. No accounting for taste, I say. I'd run a mile myself. Hello, is that Sergeant Tomkins?'

She reached out an arm and pressed the talk-out button so that they could both listen.

'I'm ringing from the Rigorous Assessment Unit. We have a strange character outside the office interfering with our clients. He's wearing a hawaiian shirt and one of those large floppy hats with corks all round it. We'd appreciate having him carted away.'

'Is he doing any harm?'

'Not physically, no.'

'You mean psychologically then. Are they freaking out?'

Gripp leaned forward and seized the telephone.

'Listen, sergeant,' he said. 'It's Greg Gripp here. Supremo. Perhaps I need to explain that the efficiency of our unit relies on an atmosphere of fear and uncertainty. We can't have people fraternising with our clients, perhaps winding them up to some kind of anti-social behaviour. We need him removed.'

'It's a question of manpower, sir. The cuts mean we're down to dire emergencies.'

'Count this as one.'

'You called us out yesterday, sir, if you remember. Little chap up a ladder with a camera supposedly terrorising the neighbourhood. Turns out he was completely legit, working for one of the newspapers we're very close to.'

'So you're refusing to come out?'

'Not refusing exactly, sir. But we've got a major alert on at the moment, which involves several of our crack teams all at once. Call us back if he hasn't gone in an hour or so.'

'Thanks for nothing,' Gripp addressed the dialling tone.

'I think that shows a reprehensible lack of respect for your position, Mr Gripp,' Ellie said. 'I am personally offended.'

His expression softened a little, and he patted her on the shoulder.

'Greg,' she corrected herself with a blush.

*

Tuesday

'It's Bodge, Terry. I thought we should have a brief chat.'

'Surprise me,' Bolt said. 'It's the Goodblow interview.'

'How perspicacious of you.'

'It sounded completely professional to me.'

'You've put your finger on it. Professional, meaning nastily cynical. Questioning the probity of Lord Botting and the British government.'

'Of the Conservative party, you mean.'

'A pointless quibble, if I may say so. Do you regard Blurt's line of questioning as in any way helpful, Terry? It seemed to me that he was totally lacking in deference.'

'That's his job.'

'For the time being, Terry.'

*

Chloe lay snugly ensconced within sheets of Egyptian cotton on a bed of such unaccustomed comfort that it seemed to caress and soothe her yielding limbs at her slightest languid movement. Squinting through half-closed eyes to avoid full wakefulness, she took in a crystal chandelier, jade table lamps with delicate silk shades, a pair of Louis XV armchairs, fabric wallcoverings, murals fleshily depicting classical themes.

She had no memory of arriving here, but when at first light she had stolen from the covers to answer a call of nature she had padded across deep carpet and pushed her face between the heaviness of the swagged curtains to see, to her joyful surprise, the Thames far below alongside a miniature Tower of London with, beyond it, St Paul's Cathedral on one side of the river and the London Eye on the other.

'Hair of the wolf,' said Freddie, arriving at the bedside with two tall glasses on a tray. 'Buck's fizz, as the Reverend Spooner might have said.'

Lady Thatcher's Wink

She sipped dreamily.

'Do you bring all your girls here?' she asked.

'You're the first.'

'Of course I don't believe you.'

'But it happens to be true,' he said. 'It belongs to my old mucker Bruno Fotheringay, and he's given me the run of it while he's behaving abominably in the Bahamas for a month.'

'A whole month!'

He laughed.

'Let's take each day as it comes,' he said, 'but I don't see any point in getting up for this one. Filthy weather outside – rain, hailstones, thunder and lightning. I shouldn't be surprised if we got deep snow later on.'

'Of course I don't believe you,' she giggled, 'but why don't you slide back in here and try to persuade me.'

*

It was bad luck for the police that they were called out too late in the morning to ramrod the carpet factory door. It stood wide open, and though Strutters for a second considered tugging it shut and commanding his men to splinter it into tiny pieces, he decided there was terror enough in the flashing lights of his five squad cars and the hoarse panting and strenuous whining of the three muscle-bound dogs which, straining on their leashes, were now urged up the metal stairs towards the owner's office. His unleashed officers, meanwhile, fine-tuned to spread fear, pounded their steel-tipped boots on each step to create an ear-splitting cacophony akin to a dozen blacksmiths simultaneously threshing their hammers on molten bars.

'What is this tumultuousness, please?' gasped the terrified Deepak Chaudhri, rising from his chair with arms held wide in surrender. 'What have I done?'

Tuesday

One of the beasts, baring its teeth, showed a keen interest in his knees.

'It's your boy we want,' Strutters said. 'Where is he?'

His posse followed the waved arm and went clattering along a corridor.

'Please, what possibly can he have done?'

Strutter unfolded a large reprint of the offending portrait and lay it on the desk.

'You recognise it?'

'I know the lady, of course. A truly great lady. But what is all this behind her?'

'Dirty pictures, Mr Chaudhri. Filthiness.'

'My goodness!' He peered closer. 'But you don't believe that my Emre drew these things?'

'Not drew them. He promulgated them. That's a word we use for this kind of thing. You know he has a blog?'

'Of course. But surely he does no harm . . .'

'Perhaps you're unaware of the sheer scale and reach of the internet, Mr Chaudhri. The material spreads like a rash, an infection. Believe me, these disgusting images are at this very moment being ogled by vulnerable eyes in every far corner of the globe.'

'Good heavens!'

'I don't know what time it is in Papua New Guinea, Mr Chaudhri, but there'll be an innocent mother waking in her grass hut to find her susceptible sons and daughters crowded round a mobile phone and eagerly gawping over this depraved picture. Depraved is another technical word we use. Some unsuspecting Arab fisherman calmly piloting his dhow through tranquil waters will be switching on his device to be assailed by this vile depiction of Mrs Thatcher and her naked companions. Depiction is a further police term, I should perhaps explain. An illiterate Patagonian cowherd, taking

Lady Thatcher's Wink

shelter from the pampas winds, will be idly flicking through his picture gallery . . .'

'But what law exactly is my Emre breaking,' the distressed carpet salesman interrupted. 'What will you charge him with?'

Strutters snorted.

'We're spoilt for choice, if I'm honest. Terrorism Supression is probably the simplest.'

'Terrorism! That hopeless boy can hardly light a match, let alone a bomb.'

'No, no, Mr Chaudhri, you obviously don't understand. I expect you've heard of the odd would-be assasssin being banged up under the Act, but if you wasted your busy time reading the clauses and sub-clauses – which naturally you won't – you'll realise that they're neatly devised to root out all sorts of nuisance people we couldn't otherwise lay a finger on. That's how the law works in this country.'

'But in this case?'

'That's easy.' He looked up to a shelf of carpet samples on the wall behind the desk and read a label aloud. 'Afghan. That's Afghanistan, I take it. Have you been there?'

'Of course. Though not for several years, in the present difficult circumstances.'

'Very difficult. A war zone. Some friends, but many more enemies. So what were you doing in Afghanistan?'

'Buying carpets.'

'A useful front, eh? Don't misunderstand me, Mr Chaudhri, we're talking about how it looks. I'm not for a moment impugning (if you'll forgive some more of our jargon) your integrity. Have your customers never given you a suspicious glance.'

'Not that I'm aware.'

'Let's consider skins, shall we? And I stress that there's not a trace of racism in the police. You're an Indian gentleman.'

Tuesday

'Anglo-Indian. But I'm British. I was born here.'

'Indian. And your lad's called Emre. That's not Indian, is it?'

'Turkish. My wife's family came from there originally.'

'Ha! Well, I'm not sure exactly where we stand politically with the Turks at the moment, but your average red-blooded Englishman will think first of scimitars, trust me on that. So now we have Indians and Turks. Any Pakistanis?'

'Some distant relatives.'

'Distant, eh? Just think how that sounds. Not honest enough to admit it openly. Distant is a weasel word, as if you've something shameful to hide. A profile is emerging.'

'This is disgraceful.'

'Just what we call circumstantial evidence, Mr Chaudhri. We'd need a bit more to convince a jury, but you can see that we're almost half way there already. The charge, in view of the insult to the late Mrs Thatcher, would probably come under the Harm to UK Reputation clause.'

At this moment there came the sound of running feet along the corridor, and the handcuffed Emre, a powerful arm under each armpit, was propelled into the room and dropped heavily to the floor. One of his cheeks was cut and already swelling into an ugly bruise.

'Hello . . . Taz,' Strutters said. 'Good to see you again.'

'He was trying to escape,' explained one of his carriers.

'Thank you, Dunnock.'

'I was sitting down,' their victim said weakly.

'Aggressively. And with a glint in his eye.'

'We have four witnesses,' Strutters said.

'It was before anyone else came into the room.'

'Four trustworthy witnesses who will swear to identical accounts on oath. Oh dear, he's trying to escape again.'

He leaned down and struck a meaty blow on the other cheek.

'This is dirty business,' he said, brandishing his copy of the portrait. He turned to Chaudhri. 'Perhaps we'll go down the pornography route after all.'

'No, no, please not that!' the poor man pleaded, wringing his hands in what Strutters regarded as a comically theatrical manner. 'That would be an indelible stain on our family.'

'You prefer terrorism?'

'At a pinch, sir. But have you nothing else?'

'Oh, we've a raft of them. Let's see how well he cooperates, shall we? Off to the station with him, boys, and let's pick up every computer and electronic gizmo in the building.'

There were tears in Chaudhri's eyes as he watched his son being manhandled as roughly as humanly possible down the stairs.

'I revered that wonderful lady,' he told the empty room. 'She was a polygon of virtue.'

*

'It's a *joke*, Alan,' Gloria said despairingly. 'Can we try it again, please? With feeling.'

They were in the unlovely ante-room of a community centre in Penge: two plastic chairs, a trestle table with chipped laminate surface, walls stuck with lopsided and almost certainly out-of-date leaflets advertising pilates classes, transmissible disease clinics and mobile library visiting times. A few steps away, in the main hall, the first two rows of stackable chairs in an optimistic phalanx of ten were beginning to fill.

'What Lady Thatcher is encouraging those young lovers to do,' he repeated in the same flat tones as before, 'is what her party is doing to you.'

She wanted to scream, but pin-pricked her beautifully varnished nails into her palms instead.

Tuesday

'You do get the point of this, Alan? What we're saying?'

'If I'm honest, we seem to be suggesting that voting Tory will guarantee people a pretty good time.'

'Oh, God.'

'But that can't be it, I suppose. Obviously not.'

'Alan, what we're saying – what you *should* be saying – what you *would* be saying if you could manage a lightness of tone and perhaps even the hint of a leer, is that we're all being *screwed* by this government.'

'Oh, I see.'

'Though of course you can't put it like that.'

'I suppose not. Shall I try again? What Lady Thatcher . . .'

'No, stop!'

'. . . is encouraging . . .'

'Please stop, Alan! My fault – you simply can't do it. Try something more pithy.' Having spent good campaign money hiring a couple of gag writers to capitalise on the portrait farce, she was determined not to fail. 'You choose.'

He consulted his sheet and took a deep breath.

'What' he asked, 'has the Tory government got in common with the Thatcher portrait?'

'Just a slight pause,' she said, 'and . . .'

A knock on the door announced a slip of a girl wearing a worried frown and a large red rosette.

'I think they're ready for us,' she said. 'If the volunteers all come in we can make up the best part of four rows.'

'We'll leave the jokes for Cockfosters,' Gloria decided, leading the way out.

She turned to see Sprout stuck to the spot, immobile but for his shoulders, which rose and fell in irrepressible mirth.

'Alan?'

'Cockfosters!' he said, shaking helplessly. 'That's a very funny name. Can we work up a joke about it?'

*

Lord Botting of Botting was in remarkably good humour considering how wickedly his generous gift had been vandalised.

'No, I don't blame the government,' he told the BBC's flagship lunchtime radio programme. 'Which of us can keep an eye on every single room in the house? I'd have to devote an hour a day to it at Botting Towers.'

'It won't make you more cautious about future donations to the party?'

'The words side, bread and buttered come to mind, my dear.' (The interviewer was a young woman he was finding rather cute.) 'Who else is going to look after my interests?'

'You've received an apology?'

'No need at all. The person I feel sorry for is poor Stretton Mathers.'

'The artist.'

'The portraitist *par excellence*, young lady, of our nation's great and good. Which of us hasn't wept before his glorious apotheosis of our late queen at the National Gallery or been moved to bend the knee to his bravura knight-in-armour treatment of our present monarch? The Thatcher daub may be a bit humbler in scale, but I commissioned it after he'd turned my own ugly mug into a thing of relative beauty for what I thought was a very reasonable fee. We're talking five figures, but that's what you pay for genius.'

'He's presumably pretty angry.'

'I'm not a squeamish man, sweetheart, but I haven't plucked up the courage to enquire. Better ask him yourself.'

*

Tuesday

'You really are a very clever girl,' Freddie murmured, adding to the accretion of empty plates and spent glasses on his bedside table. 'Memorably inventive.'

'And I make good eggs benedict, too,' she said. 'Unless by any chance that's what you were referring to.'

'You made the hollandaise?'

'Not likely – your Bruno has a well-stocked fridge. We must be sure to thank him one day.'

'I wouldn't let him near you.'

The afternoon was on its way, but only the smeared crockery marked its forward crawl.

'Tell me what my clever girl studied for her anthropollox.'

'South Sea Islanders, of course,' she said, running a delicate fingernail snake-like along his inner forearm from wrist to elbow. 'Depraved innocence.'

*

'This one's a bit near the knuckle,' Fergie Wood half apologised to the *Maul*'s editorial meeting. 'A touch of the Gillrays or Rowlandsons, I suppose.'

They all crowded round the cartoon, which showed a row of exposed buttocks. Their owners were engaged in acts which were unmistakeable, though tastefully obscure, and the heads that swivelled to face the viewer revealed the features of all the leading election candidates. Big Ben stood tall behind them, while to one side stood two caricature elderly women with shopping bags. The caption read: Where are you thinking of marking your cross, Brenda?

'Will the readers cope?' Frisby wondered aloud. 'It's bloody brilliant, Fergie.'

'The Thatcher pic will have softened them up,' Frank Bludgeon said. 'I say go for it.'

Lady Thatcher's Wink

'Harry?'

'Just to point out that, for obvious reasons, we couldn't include Valmai Partridge in the scene,' the news editor said. 'But we dropped her proud knockers from the front page this morning to make way for Maggie, so perhaps we might reinstate them tomorrow. A bit of uplift.'

'With a knocking piece, if you'll excuse the pun,' Snitch suggested. 'I assume my editorial won't be backing any of the parties this time round, Dalt.'

'Damn them all,' the editor instructed.

A tanned arm was raised in the air.

'May I suggest a revised caption for the cartoon?'

'Try me,' Frisby said.

'How about, If only we had a postal vote, Brenda?'

There was a short silence followed by a gale of laughter. Luke Freemantle had won his spurs.

*

'It's Bodge, Terry.'

'Bodge *again* Terry, you mean. The Botting interview?'

'Exactly so.'

'He couldn't have been happier. No blame attached. Even invited our young interviewer out for an evening romp, as he alluringly called it. She declined, should your department need to know. What's your beef this time?'

'Simply the fact that the BBC ran it. Lady Thatcher herself bequeathed us a useful expression. You gave the wretched story the oxygen of publicity.'

'You mean the portrait saga is out of bounds?'

'That's exactly what I mean. You've done it to death, Terry. Nobody wants any more of it. It's boring. It's not . . .'

'Helpful?'

Tuesday

'It's positively harmful.'
'Fuck off, Bodge.'

*

'Sorry to break into your exciting speech schedule, Stu,' Turtle opened with heavy irony, 'but there's been a promising new development on the Thatcher front, which Fitz will explain. I gather you've had a good deal of ribaldry to cope with out on the stump?'

'I've ignored it.'

'And my little prompts to deflect the flack towards other targets?

'I've ignored them.'

'Oh.'

'Let's move on, shall we?' Julian suggested emolliently. 'The police have been very accommodating.'

'You mean, I suppose, that they've applied the thumbscrews to that little runt of a blogger,' Turtle asked. 'I certainly hope so.'

'No, no, no, nothing physical at all. It's a digital world today, Gerry. They've traced the image to his girlfriend's phone. Bingo! as one might say.'

'Why might one say bingo?' Warbytton asked.

'The real question, Warbs, isn't why, but how. How did the little lady come to be inside these walls? And we have the answer to that, too: she's a cleaner here. Double bingo!'

'Which in itself isn't a huge advance,' Turtle added, further preparing the ground, 'although we could – I mean the police could – prefer various charges regarding national security, terms of employment, insult to a public figure and the rest. But on to the treble bingo, Fitz.'

'We have the complete profile, Warbs. Her name is Chloe

Somerville. She's twenty-four and she took one of those useless arts degrees, in her case anthropology, but . . .'

'You took an arts degree,' Warbytton broke in. 'PPE.'

'But they weren't useless then,' Turtle intervened, defending himself as well as the chief of staff. 'That was yesterday, the bad old days. Things have changed, Stu. This isn't a time for airy idealists with no experience of the real world. Why do you think the TV news bulletins are almost choked with sequences showing Lambert with a bright yellow hard-hat perched on his head, inspecting nuts-and-bolts factories as if there's nothing he'd like better than a job involving a spanner? Why do you think he's slashed university funding for anything that doesn't bring in ready cash?'

Julian raised both hands, palms down, for all the world as if to impart a blessing, but actually to silence Turtle and reclaim the initiative.

'But,' he said, 'she was originally enrolled at some minor art college. It closed down before she could start her course.'

'We closed them down,' Warbytton said.

'Indeed. But you see where this leads us?'

Warbytton didn't.

'Ah, but I've carelessly left something out. Young Chloe is missing. She's probably sheltering in some ill-favoured hideaway, prostrate with fear. Supine, even. Both in turn.'

'Which, Stu,' Turtle said, 'gives you your cue.'

'Does it?'

'For absence, read guilt,' Julian purred. 'We need to lay the blame on an outsider, and fortunately she's not here to defend herself. She's an artist! She took a photograph, we'll suggest, of dirty pictures which she herself had drawn. She was fatally proud of her scabrous handiwork. QED.'

'But Freddie's not here either,' Warbytton said. 'I thought everyone was blaming him.'

Tuesday

'The *Telegram* killed that one off this morning,' Turtle said, 'with a quote from his mother about how cack-handed he was with a paint brush. Apparently the smoke blew two ways from his chimneys.'

'What we need from you,' Julian smiled collusively, 'is the dawning recollection of having come across this scatologist at her work – although you couldn't possibly have had an idea of what she was up to at the time.'

'You expect me to . . .'

'Not to lie, Warbs, but to use your imagination. Of course if you'd actually seen her doing it you would have reported her immediately, so we have to tread a little carefully.'

'Without any evidence.'

'Naturally. How does this sound? Let's imagine that you wake up early one morning, can't sleep in the heat and so forth. You pad downstairs and nod a greeting to Mrs Mopp. She has something between her fingers which you don't recognise but idly think must be part of her cleaning kit. It's only much later, which means today, that you revisit the moment and realise that what you saw was, after all, a charcoal stick.'

'I'm to condemn this poor girl with a fiction?'

'This is a green bib we're talking about, Stu,' Turtle groaned with a despairing shake of the head. 'A Power4Us cleaning woman. She's someone who works for a pittance and can be fired at a second's notice. She's at the bottom of the pile.'

'Meaning?'

'That she's disposable, for God's sake. She doesn't matter. We simply need to get this blasted story out of our hair until the voting's over.'

'I don't think so.'

'It's too late not to think so, Stu,' Turtle said. 'Our story's out there already. I've dropped the name and the hints.'

'And you've dropped me in it too?'

Lady Thatcher's Wink

'Tangentially, Stu, tangentially.' (The word had a mellifluous vagueness he loved.) 'Someone is thought to have seen the charcoal stick in her hand. May possibly have been the PM. Still investigating the rumour, that sort of thing. Just needs firming up. Over to you. Any questions?'

'Only one. Will you please never call me Stu again? Nobody else does it, nobody has ever done it, and it's the most infantile and demeaning form of address I can imagine. Plain Warbytton will do.'

'Oh,' Turtle said.

*

'What has the Tory government got in common with the Thatcher portrait?' Sprout asked his Cockfosters audience woodenly.

Gloria counted silently: 'One, two and . . .'

But he had lost it.

'They're both in Downing Street,' an ill-mannered wag piped up, 'which you and your lot will never be.'

The applause was loud and derisory.

'Let's call it a day, Alan,' Gloria suggested.

*

'Why should I give a tinker's cuss what someone does to one of my portraits?' Stretton Mathers asked the BBC's flagship early evening radio programme. 'I'm not precious about my art, like a few wilting violets I could mention. Once I've been paid for my work a client can wipe his backside on it for all I care.'

Mathers, a writhing orange cravat coiled under his throat, a crimson smock-shirt falling over purple velour trousers, was precious only about his image.

'You don't regard it as an insult – to the sitter, if not to yourself?'

'Simply redresses the balance a little. Tones down the blatant flattery, doesn't it?'

'So these rampant nudes . . .'

'Skilfully sketched. Couldn't have drawn them better if I'd been asked to do it myself, which' (he barked a laugh at his own meagre jest) 'for some strange reason I wasn't.'

'They're not obscene?'

'A meaningless word. Do you know Titian's Two Satyrs in a Landscape?'

'I'm afraid not.'

'That's the benchmark. Naked figures in all their vigour. Now look at this sinuous line. Note the cross-hatching for these shadows. The artist who embellished my Thatcher vignette bears comparison with the master. Who on earth is he?'

'We don't know. It may be a she.'

'Even more remarkable.' (Another bark.) 'Is that sexist enough for you, darling?'

*

Monty Muckle, a microphone at his lips, was in barrow boy mode as he stalked the bustling thoroughfares of Covent Garden.

'England for the English!' he boomed. 'Would anyone here like to argue against that?'

A troupe of Chinese fire-eaters paraded past, smelling of naphtha and kerosene. Two spindly Africans sat on their haunches by a rug laden with gaudy bracelets, raffia bags and fake-branded watches, while a third kept a lookout for the law. A Bolivian trio in ponchos coaxed ethnic melodies from a charango, an Andean saxophone and a set of sheep's hoofs.

'Here's a likely voter for Excalibur,' Muckle chirped. 'What's your name, sir?'

'Meni tinch qo'ying!'

'Another one! If there's an Englishman in town, will he please step forward.'

'Racist!' called a youth from the recesses of an arcade.

'Come here and say that.'

'Racist!' he repeated, and stepped forward. 'Your party's a disgrace.'

'That's what you don't understand about us, squire,' Muckle protested. 'I have no argument with any race or any creed. Believe me, I love mankind in all its colourful guises. Bring on variety, I say. You won't find a racist bone in my body. There are just too many of them.'

A sallow-skinned giant wearing a turban, patchwork robe and sandals strode up to him and, grinning hugely, beat him on the chest.

'Hang on, Charlie!'

'Plis allow me to tell you sir,' he pointed a long finger at the image of the king on Muckle's t-shirt, 'this is great man. We love your monkey.'

'Thank you,' beamed Muckle, as if he had created the institution himself. 'I am proud to say . . .'

Whatever it was he attempted to add was drowned by the intensifying noise above their heads. It had been growing steadily for minutes, and now it was close to deafening. When he looked up he saw the sky darkened by a procession of circling airliners, stacked six deep with (he peered at distant specks) at least a dozen at each level.

It was unquestionably another aviation first.

*

Tuesday

Warbytton delivered his final speech of the day before a small and bored audience in Dollis Hill. Whom the weather failed to exhaust, his standard concatenation of lies, empty promises and pathetic bromides had soon reduced to a stunned, blank-eyed stupor, and yet he himself felt strangely energised.

'I can take questions,' he offered as the gentle rustle of applause quickly died away. 'I'd *like* to take questions.'

There was no stirring among the shrubbery of blue rosettes before him, but a coiled figure mercifully broke the silence by springing up from the front row and announcing himself as Nick Hassle from NW Radio.

'Will the prime minister confirm,' he demanded, 'that a Downing Street cleaner was responsible for defacing the Thatcher portrait?'

Warbytton summoned Turtle's useful couple of lines to mind and briskly shredded them to ticker tape.

'That's none of my concern, young man,' he said, 'but I do call into question our using Power4Us to provide staff we could very well hire ourselves. Is that thing switched on?'

'Yes.'

'Bring it closer.'

Why was he for a moment transported back to his beloved rolling acres at Eggerton Manor, giving a gentle command here, acknowledging a respectful salute there? Because, having spent six confining months cowed by his false position and Gerry Turtle's whip-in-hand ring-mastering, he found himself suddenly and deliciously stepping free, becoming his own man again, breathing clean air. Might it even be fun to be prime minister?

'This appalling company has spread its tentacles into every fissure of our national life. Once the election is over I shall strive to ensure that large swathes of its operations are stripped away and returned to public ownership.'

Lady Thatcher's Wink

He was interrupted by his anxious PPS, who ran forward at a gallop, theatrically pointed to his wrist as if it wore a watch and whispered at full volume, 'The driver is waiting, sir. Your next appointment.'

The rosettes barely stirred as they hurried outside.

'What appointment, Jonathan?'

'Sorry sir, a diversionary tactic. I thought perhaps you might regret going a little off-message.'

'No more tactics,' Warbytton said.

*

It had been the strangest day Taz could remember. Twelve hours ago he had been dragged, bleeding, from the carpet warehouse for humiliating interrogation in a cell unswabbed of the emissions of some malodorous and incontinent overnight inhabitant, and yet here he was in a warm, book-lined study, hunched over a brand new top-of-the-range computer which he was soon, in a pre-paid taxi, to take home as his very own.

'We merely need to translate this rather formal text into your own inimitable language,' the kindly gentleman smiled.

'No problem, Mr Julian. Easy shit.'

'That's the kind of thing I meant.'

He had been proud of his refusal to buckle under pressure. Although he was pretty sure that the medieval tortures itemised by Inspector Strutters were no longer in common use (he had never seen an iron maiden outside a museum), the long hours without food and water had proved a genuine temptation to mention Chloe's name. But even after they traced the photograph to her phone, he had shaken his head and refused to incriminate her. She was even lovelier in her absence and his desolation.

'What a pathetic, mixed-race little runt you are,' Strutters had challenged him. 'You don't think that this tasty bit of crumpet cares a sparrow's kneecap for you, surely? She's probably screwing some hairy hunk even as we speak.'

'Keep trying,' Taz said, and received a swipe across the back of the head where further damage wouldn't show.

And then, as grim afternoon stretched into hapless evening, he had been surprisingly whisked away across town, shown into a luxurious shower, kitted out with fresh clothes and, after the tastiest meal he could ever remember, introduced to the smarmy Fitzroy Julian. He gathered that his benefactor was something to do with government, and he presumed that it was in some sort of ministerial office he now sat, his bruised cheeks burning but otherwise feeling in remarkably good shape. More than that he thought it wise not to know.

> Just when yew thought the BBC had plunged the depths of arrogance, frenz, comes a happy revelation that they seem to have taken aboard a serious lesson.

'Shouldn't that be dat dey?' Julian suggested.
'Sorry, I'm a bit nervous.'
'Take your time.'
He made the changes and moved on.

> Praise be, dese bloods do have a smidge of conscience after all. Here, folks, courtesy exclusively of yours truly Taz, is a snatch of their so-called Head of News, Mr Terry Bolt by name, caught in the act of confessin all in some private conclave.

'Should I leave conclave?'
'Sounds right for both us of, Taz.'

> Just go to BoltBBC@blovision and suss it out for yourselfs. He admit the heavy charge of "shameful bias". Bout time we had some of dat honesty from dem traitrous shysters!

Lady Thatcher's Wink

'Nicely put, if I may say so,' Julian congratulated him. 'That's your second scoop in two days.'

*

Warbytton was changed into his pyjamas and had already swung one leg beneath the duvet when the chancellor of the exchequer rang.

'A brief chat, Sturge.'

'It's very late.'

'Gerry asked me to call. We're approaching D-Day, after all. One more day of canvassing. Must get it right.'

'Why can't he speak to me himself?'

'I believe he senses a very slight . . . frostiness, Sturge. All in his imagination, I'm sure. And in any case, I can explain some of the niceties rather better than he can. The economic realities, I mean. He's particularly worried that you may start using the n-word.'

'I only ever said darkies, and now I'm as pure of tongue as a novitiate – though they probably swear like troopers these days.'

'I mean nationalisation. You were rather outspoken in Dollis Hill.'

'Where on earth's that?'

'Where you said that some Power4Us functions might be returned to public ownership. Of course we know that's not quite what you meant.'

'I certainly thought it was when I said it.'

'Don't worry, Sturge. Gerry has explained to the media what you were really trying to say. It didn't take much spinning. Most of them will go along with it.'

'It's a despicable organisation.'

'Of course it is. Nobody's denying it. That blabbermouth

security guard, the cleaning woman who scrawled all over the Thatcher portrait . . .'

'Allegedly.'

'Allegedly, and who at the very least took a photograph which is comic fodder for every half-brained saloon bar wit the world over. And that's before we talk about the seven hundred airliners which are tonight stranded throughout the European landmass and beyond after being unable to land safely in the UK.'

'Which rather makes my point.'

'Only the despicable bit, Sturge, not the solution. Why do you think we've shipped nearly every government operation out to Power4Us?'

'Educate me, Bertie.'

'First reason: passing the buck. When they foul things up it's not our fault but theirs. We can usefully hang them out to dry – get spitting mad on the public's behalf, as you rightly did earlier on. Full marks. Of course if they keep fouling up, the public may start to ask awkward questions about why we gave them this or that responsibiity in the first place. That's when we set up a full enquiry which will take a good few months or years to dribble away. And if things get too bad – and this air traffic control business may be the last straw – we tear up their contract and give it to somebody else.'

'Which is what I was saying, I believe.'

'No, Sturge, you spoke about public ownership. That's a very different matter indeed. Highly dangerous even to think about. Very twentieth century. Power4Us are the biggest fish in the pond by far, but they're not the only one. What you meant to say, as Gerry has carefully explained, is that we're considering whether it would be better to share some of their work out among other providers.'

'We couldn't employ our own security guards and cleaners?'

Lady Thatcher's Wink

'Ah, but there we come to my second reason, Sturge: efficiency. You won't find anyone who cuts to the bone like Power4Us.'

'Cuts to the bone?'

'I mean, to express it plainly, shafts its staff. We put a job out to tender and all we have to worry about, as long as the law isn't openly flouted, is that we get a good price. They achieve that by paying as little as they can get away with to people who, because they don't know from day to day whether they'll have any work, are desperate to take anything that's offered to them. That's modern capitalism. A nationalised industry directly answerable to the public couldn't possibly compete with that. Is everything understood?'

Warbytton reached out his free hand to pat a pile of books, magazines and newspapers on his bedside table.

'I've been doing a little research, Bertie,' he said, 'and I do have a few questions, if you don't mind.'

'It's very late.'

'I've never bothered my head much with this kind of thing before, but I've discovered that our nuclear industry is run by the North Korean government.'

'It's not a trade secret, old man.'

'The post office, as we used to call it, is in the hands of the Chinese, who also own our oilfields.'

'Manage them, Sturge. The seabed is ours.'

'The trusts which run our hospitals have been sold to Saudi Arabia and the blood transfusion service to Qatar.'

'You *have* been busy.'

'Our railways are German, our water resources are Iranian and our national airline has been sold to Indonesia.'

Probus seemed to be speaking to a child.

'Let me help you join up the dots, Sturge. This is a multi-national world we inhabit. We're not little Englanders any

Tuesday

more. Power4Us can't run everything, and certainly not the biggest stuff, so we have to buy in from elsewhere. In fact we originally thought of handing air traffic control to the Russians, and recent events suggest we may have to resurrect that plan.'

'But these are all run by foreign governments, Bertie.'

'Your point?'

'That they're all state-owned industries. I'm sorry to appear dense, but you did just tell me that they can't be efficient.'

Probus laughed.

'Forgive me – so that's your little worry! I should have explained that it's specifically *British* nationalised enterprises that can't succeed.'

'We haven't got the knack of it?'

'We're ideologically opposed to it. Don't believe in the state getting involved with things that might impact on tax or get in the way of private initiative. Shrink the state! We have our friends to serve, after all. If the state has any purpose at all it's to look after the money-makers who fund the party.'

'So we don't mind if other countries' governments run things here?'

'That's up to them, isn't it? And let's face it, some of them are even bigger bastards than Power4Us. They have to dress it up a little for UK consumption, but don't even begin to ask what corners they cut to come in cheaper than we could ever manage ourselves. It makes good business sense to use them.'

'And it doesn't cost us anything?'

'Of course it does, but nothing much comes out of our current budget. They put up the finance and we give them guarantees that they'll do very nicely out of it. But that's all a long time ahead, you see. These are long-term contracts, and people soon forget. We're happy to let future generations worry their heads about that. Any other questions?'

'No.'

'So what shall I tell Gerry?'

'That I'm going to show passion tomorrow, just as he asked.'

'Good.'

'But it won't be semblance.'

WEDNESDAY

The national press, usually adroit at translating its readers' most appalling prejudices into seemingly sage advice from the editorial floor, was at a shaming loss – not so much in too many minds as in no mind at all.

Arnold Snitch, having scrapped half a dozen anaemic opening paragraphs, opted instead for pomposity.

Our great nation deserves better from its politicians than this dull parade of uninspiring mediocrities. Is it any wonder the opinion polls record that a full 50 per cent of voters are unable to make up their minds about where to cast their vote?

The Maul *says: Go with your instincts.*

'Vile as they may be,' Dalton Frisby grinned. 'At least we won't have guessed wrong.'

The *Telegram*, duty bound to flatter the interests of the City and the land-owning classes, nevertheless floundered in its attempt to pick a worthy winner.

Which party will promise to ensure the richest pickings for those who sweat hardest in the national interest? Which party will undertake to punish the unproductive many in order to reward the moral few who turn the gilded wheels of finance?

We have heard pious words from the Conservatives about austerity, but all too few of the ominous threats that are necessary to whip the labouring droves into line. The Anti-Tax Alliance rightly favours raising income from those guilty of dissident behaviour, but has worryingly refused to rule out punishment for financial misdemeanours as well as those 'blue collar' social crimes (noise nuisance, bad language, drunkenness, insults to authority and so on) which clearly merit the severest sanction. The Business First Party suffers from a surfeit of candidates with a manufacturing rather than a sound monetary background.

We can only hope that the next twenty-four hours will produce one inspirational speech, one progressive policy, that points the way towards a prosperous future for the deserving elite.

The *Blither*, hampered by its traditional espousal of a quaint socialism nobody remembered, sought in vain for inspiration.

Who will speak for the sweat-soiled worker who watches with contempt as his slacking neighbour duns a handout from the state, quaffs a free slurp at a soup kitchen or helps himself to a goody bag at a food bank? Not 'Pretty Pecs' Sprout, who has made the Labour party a laughing stock. Not our old enemy, the Tory party, which, despite its posturings, still blurs the distinction between green and orange bibs. Not the People Power party, with its unrealistic demands for a graduated tax system which would take us back to the unenterprising days of yesteryear.

Only the *Excess* had a champion to promote. It devoted no fewer than five spreads to photographs of the monarch touring his country acres. He was quoted talking about nothing more controversial than his private obsessions (organic gardening, the tarot pack, bee-keeping, homeopathy, old buildings, an ersatz eastern mysticism recognisable to no one actually raised in the orient), but readers were invited to share an admiration which bordered on the fawning.

Among the pygmies who vainly attempt to strut our national stage, one unmistakable giant stands out, one man who has never failed to give our great country his inestimable and unwavering service through every sore trial and tribulation.

It is, indeed, a travesty that, thanks to the arcane rules that stifle our democracy, the most thoughtful and philosophical mind of his generation (and one, moreover, thoroughly schooled in the affairs, apparatus and appurtenances of state) should be forced to slink like a shameful ghost into the political shadows.

Wednesday

It is clear that the Excalibur party so vigorously led by Monty Muckle would like to give His Majesty a greater role in the governance of the country which he and his predecessors have so selflessly ruled over for years immemorial – to the admiration, it should be added, of an envious world far beyond these shores.

What that role should be, Mr Muckle has not yet vouchsafed to us, but we are in no doubt that the population at large would welcome a meaningful contribution from the Palace. Today's monarchy is much changed from the distant, hidebound institution of days gone by, as our exclusive photographs vividly demonstrate, but what remains is its deep understanding of its subject people, a profound willingness to serve and an unquenchable odour of sanctity.

The images revealed a smiling elderly gentleman, stooping to pick a flower, throwing a stick for his favourite retriever, sitting formally in a wainscoted corner of his study, proudly holding a photograph of his grandchildren and generally being a good sport.

Undoubtedly the most surprising was the one that caught him precariously balanced on a unicycle, a determined man of the people. He was seen slightly from above and at something of a distance, almost as if the photographer were terrified of too close an approach.

*

'I do think Terry Bolt was behaving in a somewhat OTT manner, Jason.' Turtle's vowels almost stroked the microphone in their tone of sympathetic sincerity. 'Perhaps, who knows, he was on the juice when he said it.'

'So you discount what he said?' Blurt asked.

'By no means. He admitted the BBC's bias, didn't he? That

was merely stating the obvious, but I'm grateful that someone in a senior position at Broadcasting House has at last admitted it. We needed that confession. It's helpful.'

'But giving up political interviewing?'

Turtle laughed gently.

'That's what I mean about the exaggeration. Of course we wouldn't want to stop that altogether. I think you'll find that the next Conservative government will sit down with the broadcasters to find a useful compromise. Perhaps a closer working with the Neutrality Overseer.'

'How would that work?'

'Perhaps news bulletins to be shown to the overseer before they go out. An agreement on what can be aired in a live interview like this one. That kind of thing.'

'Censorship.'

'No, of course not. We're proud to say that this is a free country and will always remain so. Negotiation.'

'I'd call that censorship.'

'I'm sure you would.'

'And you're pleased that Terry Bolt has resigned?'

'I do have some small sadness about it at the human level, but it was inevitable. There are limits to what can be tolerated, after all. He had to go.'

He threw a disarming smile.

'When will *you* be leaving, Jason?'

*

The nine beats of Big Ben penetrated the triple-glazed glass and thick curtains as tiny thuds.

'You do seem to have an endless supply,' Chloe said.

'And of Buck's Fizz,' Freddie grinned.

'Rather naughty.'

Wednesday

They clinked rims. Rows of smeared flutes and crumbed plates stretched away on either side of the bed. She lay back and allowed the liquid to run down her throat.

'I wonder if anyone's missing us,' she said when she came up for air.

'They certainly don't know *what* they're missing.'

Their glasses deposited, they rolled back into the middle of the bed.

'And now, Frisky Freddy,' she chided, firmly depositing a pillow between them, 'it really is time we snatched a few hours sleep.'

*

Warbytton's first speech of the day was at Hackney town hall, enticingly billed by Turtle as 'enemy territory'. By a stroke of good fortune Jessica's Galapagos reptile was engaged on various nefarious errands elsewhere – 'Putting the BBC to rights on four separate channels,' he had all but chortled – so leaving the earnest Jonathan as his lone supporter.

The Tory faithful were evidently also engaged elsewhere, for it was immediately obvious that the chippy shirt-sleeved men and cropped-haired, dungareed women who comprised most of his scant audience were of other persuasions and bristling for a fight.

'Poverty kills!' came a shrill cry before he had even opened his mouth.

'Feed our children!'

'Reward our sweat!'

Warbytton had an equally powerful arsenal of punchy slogans at his disposal but had made a vow to himself never to utter a single one of them ever again. The trouble was that he didn't otherwise know quite how to begin.

Lady Thatcher's Wink

'Friends...'

'We know who your friends are, matey!'

'Lock up all the bankers!'

Family mythology had never meant much to him, but at this moment, and just in time, he recalled the heroism of Struthers Warbytton, his grandfather with a great or two in front, famed for facing down a gang of rural toughs after his enclosure of the common woods and fields which were to become Eggerton Chase. They had swarmed into the grounds with staves and flaming torches, bent on razing the Hall, while the brazenly threatened lord of the manor, newly returned from a shoot, was armed with nothing more menacing than a brace of pheasant.

'Enough!' he had roared, as Warbytton did now.

Boldly taking the initiative, he had stepped forward to take on his assailants one by one, verbally but ruthlessly, until they had turned tail and slouched sheepishly back to their hovels.

'I promise you a new party of the people,' his grandson with a great or two in front now declared (much, no doubt, to the fury of that ancient shade), and pointed towards a young woman with purple hair. 'Ask me a question.'

'How does a poncey toff like you dare stand up there and look the likes of us in the face?' she demanded.

'Because,' he told her, metaphorically waving a pair of gamebirds before her eyes, 'I have witnessed your suffering at first hand. I have been to the food banks and the benefit queues. And I mean to do something about it. Next!'

'Where are the jobs your lot promised? Why are hospitals shutting their doors to those who can't afford to pay?'

'We have turned our backs on the needy millions,' he said, surprised to find himself waving a fist in the air. 'If you re-elect me as prime minister I shall ensure that a reborn Conservative party will create a society that is fair for all.'

Wednesday

He glanced behind him to see the face of his young PPS chalk white and contorted in horror, a parody of the famous Edvard Munch painting. Right on cue, the mouth gaped wide in a comical O.

Yes, everything was going swimmingly.

*

'What's your game, Gerry?'

'Game, Gloria? As if I would.'

He took the call as he left the potted palms and comfortable purple sofa of his favourite commercial TV company. They had been generously accommodating, unctuously delighted by his attack on their monolithic rival, but the evils of the BBC had suddenly become a sideshow.

'Your man's gone stark-staring native.'

'The semblance of . . .'

'No, Gerry, the reality of. He's actually been quoting Karl Marx. As I assume you know.'

'Of course I do.'

'This isn't some cunning ploy of yours? To pick up some crazed lefty votes at the last minute?'

'What do you think, Gloria?'

They were for a moment by the water cooler in the offices of the *Ham & High*, colleagues drawn close together by some stupid decision of the editor or the board, by life's despicable cussedness. Two against the world.

'That's what I thought,' she said. 'I'm sorry, Gerry.'

He laughed painfully.

'But not too sorry, I suppose.'

'Professionally, no. You know full well what I'm going to have to do.'

'Naturally, Gloria. I'd do exactly the same myself.'

'Have you noticed anything about the way our clients are behaving this morning? Greg?'

It still seemed such a forward thing to call so wonderful a man by his Christian name. First name. (She couldn't get used to that, either.)

'I try not to catch their vibes. Keep a distance, Ellie.'

'They're a bit uppity, to my mind. One of them said things may be about to change. Don't know what's got into them.'

'Nothing's going to change.'

'Something about a fairer society.'

He drew himself up.

'If anyone mentions fairness,' he instructed her, 'you take them straight off handouts, no questions asked. It was fairness that got this country into a mess in the first place.'

*

He had never seen such a clamour. His second meeting of the day had taken him (he had no reason to doubt Jonathan's grasp of geography) to the Enfield civic centre, where the aisles were overflowing and an eager rabble thronged round the makeshift stage as if he were a rock star.

'Forgive me for troubling,' the PPS said wanly as they gazed down upon the multitude, 'but Mr Turtle is asking that you stick to the script this time.'

'Asking?'

'Begging. I don't think you appreciate.'

'But I *do*, Jonathan. Isn't that the joy of it?'

A good third of the audience were reporters of one kind or another. They crouched over laptops, manned tripods topped by vastly expensive cameras, held at arm's length unwieldy boom microphones swathed in foam, chattered excitedly into mobile telephones. One little fellow, who must have bagged his vantage place well in advance, was perched above the melée on a stepladder and thrust his camera forward almost into Warbytton's face.

'Please, sir!' Jonathan hissed in desperation. 'I'm afraid that Mr Turtle may lay some of the blame on me.'

'Nonsense, my boy!' Warbytton grinned. 'You have nothing to lose but your chains.'

Just as he was about to speak, four young men, presumably rival hacks, sprang forward, grasped the stepladder in firm hands and barged their way through the crowd to deposit the contraption, its inhabitant perched quivering on a high rung, in a far corner of the room. This feat was met with hearty applause.

'Friends,' he began, and this time not a soul interrupted. 'As a great man once said, the rich will do anything for the poor but get off their backs.'

The flashlights stinging his eyes, he extemporised with an unaccustomed passion from his recent nighttime reading. His own chains had fallen away.

*

'I hate to see you trussed up like this, Applied Mathematics,' Daphne said. 'But you can't say you wasn't warned, can you?'

'Nrrrrr,' he replied through his bandages.

'That's your fourth little mishap to my reckoning on that mistake of a vehicle.'

'Fifff,' he corrected her, his face contorted in pain.

He lay on the hospital bed, both legs in plaster and held up high in a hoist, an intravenous drip stuck in one arm, his flesh swaddled in dressings.

'The girls all send best wishes, except for Anthropology Two. Nobody's seen hair nor hide of her for two mornings. She's in the Power4Us condemnation book for certain – may never work again. What happened to you this time?'

'Fffried toovrttake.'

'What?'

'A buzz.'

'I've no patience,' Daphne said. 'But here's a bag of treats for when you're feeling better. Just promise me you'll never get on one of those things again.'

He groaned: 'Wanna die!'

She stood to leave.

'Well, you're getting closer to it every time,' she said. 'Sixth time lucky.'

*

Alan Sprout sipped a glass of water and prepared to try his revamped credo on a bored audience in Hillingdon. In truth he found the new role easier to perform. It had always been tricky having to attack the Tories as scoundrels while merely finessing their policies. Now their leader seemed to be taking them in a new direction altogether.

'They've vacated the centre ground, Alan!' Gloria had gushed when news of Warbytton's surprising conversion broke earlier in the day. 'That's ours now. We've a day to make it count.'

The old scripts had been torn up and replaced, with an eye on the clock, by a few necessarily short alternatives.

'But can we make Working Employees to the Bone a Labour slogan?' he had asked, remembering his union background. 'I mean, we used to stand for something rather different.'

'All those years ago? Of course, but these labels are just a polite fiction, aren't they? The Conservatives have fracked and built all over the green belt, sold everything off to foreigners and beggared our schools and the national health service, but they still pretend that they care about keeping things as they were. Our own conceit is caring about working people, but everyone knows that we don't really. It's a matter of getting into power and then doing the best we can with it.'

'Whatever best means.'

'Quite. It means whatever we want it to mean.'

Learning his new lines in short order was out of the question for the ponderous Sprout, but the hall was blessed with a system which allowed the rigging up of an autocue, with the omnicompetent Gloria pressing the buttons for him.

'Labour promises you a new crack-down on orange-vest parasites,' he began. 'We pledge to phase out all handouts by the end of the next parliament. Let skivers find work or beg for their living!'

He paused to assess the reaction. There were, he had to acknowledge, some surprised faces in his audience, but a few scattered handclaps encouraged him to press on.

'Those who won't sweat shan't vote. The franchise will be withdrawn from all orange vests immediately and from green vests who have been soaking up handouts for three years.

'We shall build a land fit for the ruthless heroes who drive our economy, unshackling them from outdated red tape which, incredibly, still gives low-grade workers arcane health and safety rights in their workplaces.

'A Labour government will strengthen the notoriously weak Tory anti-terrorism measures, installing cameras and microphones in the homes and cars of those individuals the authorities regard as potential disturbers of the peace.'

The slamming of doors advertised the disgruntlement of a few who could take no more, but Sprout was encouraged to see several red-rosettes on their feet and holding their arms out in acclaim, as if swooning converts at some revivalist meeting. Gloria Brightbloom, for her part, beamed with pleasure and raised two thumbs in the air.

'A new dawn!' she mouthed.

*

The Pink Party leader appraised her former prime selling points on the *Maul*'s front page with rueful pleasure.

'But they're still quite pert, aren't they, Duggie?'

'They're a treat, Vavoomshka,' said her fourth husband, who specialised in inventive endearments. 'I wouldn't swap them for anyone else's. Even if I had the chance these days.'

'But Game Bird Partridge is a bit much, don't you think? They're suggesting I've got a dirty past. Who do they think they are? Voracious Valmai!'

'Well, you *were* a call-girl.'

'An escort, Duggie. Respectable. No hanky-panky unless I initiated it. Which of course . . . Could I sue them?'

'They'd have you for breakfast.'

She gave the filthiest of laughs.

'They wouldn't be the first, Duggie!'

*

Monty Muckle settled into the ample cushions of the studio's purple sofa, feeling even more puppishly buoyant than usual. The make-up girl's adulation had tickled him even more than her powder brush ('You've really got those dodgy foreigners wetting themselves, Mr M!'), but it was as nothing compared with the morning's strange political contortions. He couldn't believe his luck.

Wednesday

'Who hasn't had enough of these career politicians?' he demanded. 'Pissed off is the technical expression.'

'Ha, ha! I don't think . . .'

The lunchtime programme was supposed to be a chummy affair, and its milk-and-water presenting duo, Hugh Smythe and Miranda Glew, were at their happiest coaxing behind-the-scenes tales from the stars of stage and screen. They loved mutual simpering and frankly hated election seasons.

'No, Hugh, that's not the way they normally talk, is it? They're speaking clocks. They've had no experience of life at the coalface. But I've been round the block. I was a chicken sexer, you know. I expect you've done your research. Have you ever sexed a chicken?'

'No,' said Smythe, who had been given the cuttings but hadn't bothered to read them.

'Shall I show you how it's done?' (He began to mime.) 'Nimble fingers.'

'We'd rather not, I think.'

They laughed conspiratorially. This was much more their scene. Wasn't it Jack Nicholson who had told them some tale about handling the nether parts of an animal? Or perhaps it was Brad Pitt.

'And I've been a night club bouncer. I don't suppose you'd like a demonstration of that, either. Me assuming you're the boozed-up trouble-maker, I mean.' (He rolled up a sleeve.) 'Brawny fists.'

'But you're a mortician yourself,' Glew said, responding to a prompt in her earplug. That couldn't be right. 'Politician.'

'Nonsense. I'm a man of the people, who knows what the people want. That's why Excalibur is shooting up the charts. Have you seen the latest opinion polls? Of course you have!'

'Critics say your only policy is being nasty to elephants.'

'What?'

'Immigrants.' (God in heaven, she had *twice* asked for the battery to be replaced.)

Muckle seemed cruelly offended.

'We're never nasty. We just say they should know their place. Look, I was a barrow boy – as I'm sure your research has shown you. I can't think how many pounds of spuds and oranges I sold to our coloured brethren during those years, and always with a smile and a quip, as long as they behaved right. Course, it was another matter if they didn't.'

He leaned forward conspiratorially.

'And may I remind you who our party puts up on a lofty pedestal?'

'I think you mean the king,' said Smythe, who had at least researched that much.

'Yes, our blessed monarch! Has your research shown you that there's more than a trace of the German and the Greek in his royal blood? A little known fact perhaps, and just a tad regrettable, but it's true. And yet we and the population at large absolutely revere him! Why? Because he and his family have turned their backs on all that and become thoroughly English. That's all we ask of johnny foreigner when it comes down to it.'

'But your fallacy . . . policy . . .' Glew (and her frustrated producer) tried again.

'If you want policy,' he almost exploded, 'I'll give it to you! Have you seen the way those Tory and Labour shucksters have been chopping and changing their tunes today? Adolf Lenin meets Vladimir Hitler! You wouldn't trust them with your kiddy's piggybank, would you? Shall I give you a policy?'

'Try us.'

'Then this is what Excalibur will do when it wins power tomorrow: we'll give the Crown a new role in the running of the country.'

'Jeez,' faltered Glew, unprompted. Despite lacking a current

Wednesday

affairs background, she sensed that the programme might be about to break a genuine news story. 'I mean, how?'

'First *Why*. Because our king is the one figure the public trusts, always above the fray and always decent and honest. Would you disagree with that, Miranda?'

Glew's earphone now offered nothing but a crackle.

'I take your silence for a no. And then *How*. What we would do is hand the House of Lords over to the sovereign. It's a simple division, isn't it? The House of Commons stays just as it is, only of course with our Excalibur majority in it, while the king is in charge of what I think they call the other place. He can play around with it just as he chooses. It's called the Lords, for heaven's sake. The clue's in the name. Let's have the ordinary people and our supreme leader working together for the common good. Does that make sense?

'I take your silence for a yes.'

*

It was a severe dressing down. It was up before the beak. It was a hundred lines and a birching. It was the firing squad. And Warbytton didn't care.

'This can't go on, Warbs,' Fitzroy Julian said softly. 'It makes a mockery of everything we stand for.'

'The royal we,' Warbytton said.

'I think you'll find, Sturge,' Lambert Probus corrected, 'that there's universal revulsion about what you've been saying today. It simply chills the blood.'

Gerry Turtle, the fourth occupant of the Thatcher room, said nothing but nodded violently in agreement. He felt his life unravelling.

'It may be too much to hope,' Julian said, 'but is there any chance that you've had your little joke and it's all over?'

'No.'

'I thought not.'

'And I can't stay long, I'm afraid. My next meeting's in Trafalgar Square at two o'clock.'

'Your *last* meeting,' Turtle said.

'I don't think so.'

'We can't very well close a public space, but I've rung up all the other venues and cancelled. I have to warn you . . . Warbytton . . . that from now on we're into damage limitation, and you may find that very painful.'

The Thatcher portrait was back on the wall, still in all its orgiastic glory. Warbytton gazed at it fondly. It held pleasant memories.

'The public will think we're going soft in the head,' Julian said. 'All that . . . socialist claptrap.'

'I thought it went down rather well myself. Quite a bit of cheering, actually. I had a much better reception than when I was reading out that Powerpoint guff.'

'But that was safe, don't you understand? It wasn't making demands of people. More important, it wasn't making demands of *us*. Why give voters ideas?'

'Perhaps because a lot of them are having a bad time, and we could do something about it.'

Julian sighed.

'Only if we're in power, Warbs, on the unlikely assumption that we really did want to do anything like that. Please explain, Bertie. I'm exhausted already.'

'I think the real trouble, Sturge,' Probus said in as kindly a voice as he could manage, 'is that you've led a sheltered life up there at Eggerton Hall. Lovely place, and there's no reason at all why you shouldn't simply enjoy the luxuries and all that. Quite natural. But what it means is that you don't understand how ordinary people rub along.'

Wednesday

'I thought that's what I was just getting the hang of.'

'No, all you've done is concentrate on what you perceive as their sufferings. As if they want, or deserve, the same things as we do. Boo hoo, and all that. But we're talking about votes.'

'But won't they vote for us if we offer to help them?'

'Who's *they*?'

'Well, I suppose it's what someone once called the huddled masses, though I don't imagine the term will have any appeal for you.'

Probus laughed.

'It doesn't work like that, Sturge. We've spent a generation making sure that it doesn't work like that. What you're talking about is some kind of solidarity, but it doesn't exist. It's every man for himself. And woman, of course. And that's how the children will grow up, too, unless we lose our nerve.'

'You must have seen how green bibs hate orange bibs,' Julian added. 'Every worker thinks he deserves whatever he's got and despises anyone who hasn't. Everyone thinks there's a slacker behind him trying to take his job or to cheat him of handouts.'

'So if you offer to help the deprived,' Probus went on, 'your average worker thinks you're talking about someone further down the food chain who doesn't deserve it at all. He won't want any part of that. Far better to talk about rewarding sweat, and then he's sure you're talking about him.'

'Perhaps we should educate them.'

'But that's just what we *have* been doing.' He gestured towards the portrait. 'Ever since the iron lady came along. She's still giving us the wink.'

There was a tentative knock on the door and Warbytton's young PPS came in.

'Sorry to interrupt,' he said, 'but there's a bit of a kerfuffle downstairs. Your son has turned up, sir, and he's with the young cleaning woman who's been accused of defacing the portrait. The police are here.'

'Oh, shit!' Turtle groaned. 'That's all we need. Now she'll deny everything and we're back where we started.'

'She's singing.'

'That hardly seems appropriate,' Julian said. 'Perhaps it's to calm her nerves.'

'I mean she's spilling the beans.' If asked, he'd have said that Dashiell Hammett was his writer of choice, but he did read impressively widely in the genre. 'She's confessed to doing it.'

'Rejoice!' enthused Turtle. 'Quadruple bingo!'

'The police are asking whether we want to press charges.'

'God no,' Turtle said. 'Sub judice and all that. We want that wretched girl . . .'

'To keep singing?'

'Like a canary, I think you'd say, Jonathan. I'll alert the media and we'll fix her up with an early spot on TV.'

*

Warbytton knew that the party had disowned him when he arrived at Trafalgar Square to find an abandoned campaign dais just below the steps to the National Gallery. Nobody had been sent to help him. A trestle table covered by a blue cloth stitched with the Tory logo held a pile of campaign leaflets anchored by an empty beer glass, a roll of gaffer tape, a pair of scissors and, lying on its side, a silver coloured microphone. He found the switch and heard a reassuring crackle.

He was a little early. Knots of reporters idly watched him from a distance, and a scattering of blue rosettes shuffled almost reluctantly in his direction. He registered, too, groups of orange-vested young men pirouetting casually on their wheels, for all the world like unicrim gangs without their masks.

Wednesday

'Comrades!' he began.

Before he could utter another word he was almost swept off his feet by a bevy of energetic young women dressed as American cheer-leaders, who bounded forward to leap on his low platform, each shaking a large blue pompom in one hand and a red one in the other. As they formed a line behind him, two more climbed the gallery steps and unfurled a banner reading RED WARBIE ROCKS! There was something faintly familiar about them, he thought. And then they all began to chant.

'Warbie, Warbie, Warbie!' went up their cry. 'Warbie, Warbie rocks!'

When he turned back to the square he saw that another member of their troupe, displaying great enterprise and pluck, had climbed on to the famous empty plinth in the north-west corner. She clutched a stout pole topped by an immense placard which instructed the world below

> VOTE
> WARBYTTON!
> MAKE
> BLUE
> RED!

The media had already formed a jostling scrum. They swept forward, crouching and kneeling a few feet in front of him, snapping the bewilderment on his face and the colourful backdrop of bouncing, carolling girls.

'Warbie, Warbie rocks!' was all their refrain.

Among the pack of newshounds he saw the little chap who had pointed his lens so close to him at Enfield earlier in the day. He was hopping about in search of a vantage point, but every time he squeezed through to the front or poked his face and camera between someone's legs a flat hand would appear and thrust him back into the darkness again.

Lady Thatcher's Wink

And then the attack began. Unicrims or not, the young blades on their wheels meant mischief and harm. An egg was the first weapon to hit him, and then a tomato, but as he raised his arms in front of him something sharp caught him on a cheek and he was aware of a volley of stones.

As the unicycles weaved and threaded closer, Warbytton's energetic chorus line became his rescue party. The girls behind him hurried him off the dais, while those holding the banner rushed down the steps, wrapped it round the rest of the party and began a dash for safety. He half ran and was half carried until, panting heavily, he was released from his confinement at the foot of the empty plinth. Their attackers seemed to have lost interest.

'Red Warbie rocks!' called a merry voice from above his head, and he raised his eyes to the placard holder on her emnence.

'Hi, daddy!'

'Diana!'

'You made me so proud of you that I knew I just had to bring the girls down in support. You remember Serena?'

She pointed down towards a mass of blonde curls. They belonged to one of the banner carriers.

'From my cucumber diet days. We fasted ourselves to eight and a half stone before the scientists discovered that the pips jiggered the digestive tract.'

'Allegedly,' Serena said. Her womanly curves suggested a subsequent conversion to more substantial fare. 'You forgot to mention that I finished two pounds lighter than you.'

'And Popsy?' The other banner girl's heavy-framed, thick-lensed glasses and firmly set mouth gave her a severe, academic mien. 'She stayed with us that weekend the Yogic Sisterhood camped in our garden. Peace, love and beauty.'

'Was that the time all our silver cutlery went missing?'

Warbytton asked. 'Or perhaps it was occasion we had to call the police after two of the swamis took knives to each other over the favours of a priestess? A local trainee librarian, if my memory serves me.'

'They both rang around their spiritually compatible friends,' Diana said, ignoring him as she usually did, 'and we had a lovely time making the pompoms and everything on the way down in the train. In the quiet carriage, too. You should have seen the looks we got.'

'Such fun!' both girls said in unison.

Warbytton's neck was aching.

'How did you manage to get up there?' he asked.

'Easy, daddy,' she said. 'Keep it to yourself, but I liberated that handy step-ladder.'

*

Turmoil and ferment were the words on everybody's lips. It was suddenly impossible to be sure what game the politicians were playing or whether it was a game at all.

Conservative head office were taking frantic calls from their candidates in the field, asking whether they were supposed to change their slogans when making their last-minute knockings on the door. Were quotations from *Das Kapital* now to be part of their spiel and, if so, would someone please explain what surplus value, objectification and commodity fetishism were supposed to mean when they were at home? They were fiercely assured that nothing had really changed at all, but the more liberally minded among them seized an opportunity to backtrack on what they saw as the the party's worst excesses, and the message became more mixed than ever.

Labour candidates calling Smith Square were generally eager to be let off the leash, having been forced for so long to pretend that they hated everything the Tories espoused. It was wonderful to be allowed to attack the poor and defenceless for their abject weakness, but how far could they go? Capital punishment was presumably back on the agenda for serious crimes, but might the inflicting of physical as well as financial pain be floatable as a just response to antisocial behaviour? The word from Gloria Brightbloom was that no blood-curdling nostrum should be rejected as long as due consideration was given to the sensibilities of the particular electorate being canvassed. Charity, after all, generally drew fewer votes than a carefully expressed cruelty.

The public at large flooded the internet with feverish fear and excitement, share prices went into free-fall on the stock exchange and not a few clerics, making notes for their Sunday sermons, turned to the Book of Revelation and the Doctrine of Last Things.

*

'Eggie, are you all right?'

'Never felt better, Jessie. A spring in the heels. Life in the old dog yet, and that sort of thing.'

'I meant . . . in the head.'

'Ah! You've been following the election.'

'Of course not. What do you take me for?'

'People haven't been talking about it? Bit of a surprise and all that?'

'To tell the truth, Eggie, it's been the strangest day. People haven't been talking to me at all. Whenever I've opened my mouth to speak they've rushed away for some emergency or other. Dolly Ickfold's daughter went into premature labour, although she only announced the pregnancy last week, Mrs Crabtree remembered leaving a bottle of paraffin on the

Wednesday

kitchen table and had the horrible feeling that her eccentric husband was about to burn the house down, and Ted Doughty at the hardware shop dashed off to hospital after practically amputating his finger with a stanley knife in front of my eyes. He calls himself a professional, but I've never seen such a clumsy manouevre in my life. And then your doctor rang.'

'Herbert Philpott?'

'No, not old Pisspot, Eggie. Not *our* doctor, but *yours*. At Downing Street.'

'But I haven't got one.'

'You must have.'

'Well, there may be one, but I've never met him.'

'Her. Are you sure you haven't had a consultation? In which year did the first world war start?'

'1914.'

'What day of the week is it?'

'Wednesday. Why do you ask?'

'Standard questions for memory loss, Eggie. Who's the prime minister?'

Warbytton laughed.

'Ask me tomorrow night,' he said. 'What on earth is this all about?'

'She said you'd been to see her, but that she couldn't find your records. She asked me to confirm that you'd had . . . episodes.'

'As in a soap opera?'

'As in mental disturbances, Eggie. In short, she wanted to know if you'd ever been a bit wonky.'

'And what did you tell her?'

'I assured her that there's never been much going on in there at all.'

'A complete fake, Jessie, believe me.'

'It's true that she did sound rather young. She started off

with a "Mrs Eggerton, yeah?" and when I agreed she said "Cool!" But why would anyone pretend to be your doctor?'

'Because they're out to get me.'

There was a long silence.

'Dear God,' Jessie said at last. 'My poor Eggie. And I don't know the questions for paranoia.'

*

His researchers were going to get it in the neck, Matt Oberon decided. The programme was nothing without controversy, but the cameras were filming a frigging love-in.

'Such an assured control of line,' Stretton Mathers was gushing. 'A fine awareness of the medium.'

Chloe Somerville was undoubtedly a tasty adornment of the studio's rather severe ambience (the phrase *bella figura* alighted on his brain and lodged there) but she should be up against the wall (*figuratively, figuratively!* he assured himself) over her criminal vandalising of the Thatcher picture. He had valiantly attempted an opening thrust of that kind, only for Mathers to cut across him and pat her encouragingly on the knee. Hadn't the idiots seen him showboating on the other channel? Didn't they know what a preening old fart he was?

'Let's see a few more you've brought in,' he oozed. 'Ah, yes. That's egg tempera, isn't it?'

The infamous portrait had appeared fleetingly in the opening seconds, but the shameless Chloe had arrived clutching a large portfolio of drawings and paintings, and Mathers was intent on helping her show them off. They were on the fourth already.

'Bring the camera here,' he commanded, completely at home in his surroundings. The camera obeyed. 'Focus here – on this bunch of foliage.' He glanced up at the monitor. 'Just a little to the left. That's it. You see the sun flecks on the leaf?'

'It actually flexes?' Oberon asked, bewildered and prepared to be impressed. Egg tempera and scrambled eggs were all the same to him. He concentrated his gaze. 'I suppose it does rather look as if it's moving.'

Mathers ignored him and unrolled another painting. The two artists continued to trade technical terms, share abstruse confidences and enthuse about subtle hues for far too many long-drawn minutes until, mercifully, he was signalled to bring the whole sorry business to an end.

'So good of you not to interrupt us,' Mathers thanked him fulsomely as the advertisements ran. '*Do* ask us in again.'

He accompanied Chloe outside and hailed a taxi.

'I don't have many etchings, I'm afraid,' he told her, 'but why don't you come up and see what else I've got?'

*

By the time Alan Sprout was ready to give his last speech of the campaign his friends and enemies alike were ready, and distinctly more than willing, to give him a rousing welcome. They had, he observed nervously, itchy feet. They were already jostling and elbowing, spoiling for action.

It was early evening, and the air was still pleasantly warm. He mounted a raised platform on the South Bank, under the watchful gaze of the London Eye and its podloads of tourists, who were doubtless in awe of experiencing British democracy at its virile best.

A tall, suited man with a flapping Power4Us tie strode out of the crowd and gave Sprout a handshake that almost broke his fingers.

'The name's Gripp,' he said. 'I'd like to congratulate you on your latest speech.'

'You're a Labour supporter?'

'I'm a free spirit, Mr Sprout, and I'll back anyone who pledges to inflict pain with justice.'

'That's a good phrase!' Gloria broke in. 'We could use it.'

'Then make that extreme pain with justice,' Gripp offered. 'I work in handouts refusal and this is a crucial moment in whipping the idle population into line. Believe me, I've seen the future and it shirks.'

'Ooh,' said Gloria. 'Ditto. Do you have any fresh ideas we could put out there? We're running out of time.'

'Yes, extend the bib system to include wives and partners at home. Perhaps scarlet as the colour of shame.'

'But they don't draw handouts, do they?' queried Gloria, who prided herself on a mastery of regulatory minutiae.

'Precisely. We have to move into new areas to enforce our message. What are they doing sitting idly at home when they could be sweating for the nation?'

He turned away, waving a hand in farewell.

'And I'd bring back the stocks, complete with some serious ammunition.'

The police were everywhere, but Ben Strutters and his team had secured the best position for their water cannon, hard up against the embankment wall with a good view of the troublemakers.

'If there are any,' young Dunnock said innocently.

'If there aren't any,' Strutters said, 'I'll tender my resignation in the morning.' Resignations always had to be tendered. 'This is not only going to be great fun, PC Dunnock, but also highly educational for you. I don't think you've had a go at these waterworks before, have you?'

'It's always been a dream, sir. I understand they're pleasingly vicious.'

'They can down a bull moose from twenty yards. More important, they'll bowl a miscreant off his feet and plaster him against the nearest wall. For which read, where necessary, her and her.'

'We don't discriminate?'

'I do sometimes wonder whether you ever passed through police college, PC Dunnock. Discrimination is now a dirty word. It's a sackable offence. That means we have to be as aggressive, not to say brutal, to women as we are to men.'

'And children?'

'Don't complicate matters, constable. Just think how it would look if a picture of a kid you'd squashed ended up on the front page of the *Daily Maul*. Are we clear now?'

'I can't wait, inspector.'

Big Ben chimed seven times. A flock of startled pigeons, which never seemed to learn, fluttered over the river and joined Sprout's audience.

'Don't sweat, shan't vote!' he declared as an opener.

Gloria passed him a sheet of paper.

'Pain with justice!'

'Forget the justice!' a woman close at hand shouted.

'Fascist pig!' countered another, and slapped her round the face.

There were very few rosettes on display. It was a mercy to the nervous Sprout, terrified of inspiring a riot, that friends and foes were indistinguishable unless they took the risk of piping up. It was a curse to Strutters, who was looking for a clear and unmissable target, although he didn't doubt he could justify a wholesale hosing down if nothing better came along.

And then things changed.

'Let skivers starve!' Sprout bawled, and at once small groups of angry young men, some vested and some in mufti, pushed their way to the front, where they formed a fists-raised, chanting army – champions, he realised with a grateful gulp (he had been about to run for his life), of his noble cause.

'Let skivers starve!' they echoed.

While neutrals retreated and cowered, gung-ho rivals fused into their own brigade, yelling colourful abuse. Battle lines had been drawn. At which moment a conga line of scantily dressed young women took all the attention, skipping daintily towards the action along the top of the wall. The pompoms they had fluttered in Trafalgar Square that afternoon were now firmly attached to their rumps, and each held a small placard reading RED TORIES FOR WARBYTTON.

The baying mobs were struck dumb, the only sound being a couple of shrieking and indecorous wolf whistles. As the girls drew closer it was apparent that they had two male hangers-on. The first was a young man who, judging by his gait, was either stupidly hamming it up or much the worse for alcoholic wear.

'Jesus!' breathed Strutters. 'That's the Warbytton kid. I've always wanted to get one over him.'

The second, labouring to keep up with those in front, was a stout middle-aged man in shorts and sandals whose face was hidden by a pair of ridiculously large sunglasses and a floppy Australian bush hat.

Peace was short-lived. The newcomers jumped off the wall to confront Sprout's storm-troopers, waving their placards and wiggling their pompoms. Factions opposed both to Labour and to Tories of any colour coalesced into a third force, and in no time at all fists were flying, wastebins were torn from their mountings as weapons, and a heritage paving stone with lines by Wordsworth (*O, glide, fair stream! Forever so/Thy quiet soul on all bestowing*) was prised up and thrown at the police.

'Who do we target, sir?' Dunnock asked with bright eyes.

'The rule is always those furthest to the left,' Strutters said. 'Meaning, of course, political left. But in this case there's no argument at all. We go for Fuckwit Freddie and his little entourage.'

Wednesday

It was, as promised, a wonderful occasion. The deluge gun took its victims, including (unfortunate collateral damage) six passing members of a trade delegation from Uzbekistan, completely by surprise. They were first knocked off their feet, next bounced up and down by the powerful blast and finally swept, limbs flailing, into a narrow culvert, the relentless volley of water forcing them to gulp and strain for air.

Further downstream, where the flood frothed and gurgled into a drain, passers-by later saw a heap of bedraggled pom-poms, a pair of heavy-rimmed, bottle-glass spectacles, a green passport with cyrillic script on the cover and a sodden hat with bobbing corks.

*

Dalton Frisby was in a foul mood. Sitting on the fence was bad enough when the *Maul* was supposed to be setting the national agenda, but you only had to dip into the online world to know that every other Tom, Dick and Mary had a view as extreme as any of your own, and often more wittily expressed.

Worse still, his few political certainties were – and by the very hour – fragmenting like the coloured shapes shaken into new patterns by the kaleidoscopes he had played with as a boy.

'Tory hopes go up in smoke, Harry?' he suggested to his news editor.

He had already rewritten the front page headline three times, and had similarly faltered over a dozen photographs. The way the evening's mayhem was intensifying he would have more of them to choose from yet.

'We need to firm up that it's arson, Dalt. Tory HQ flames red?'

The picture showed Conservative offices ravaged by fire alongside a 'Welcome to our friendly market town' tourist sign.

Lady Thatcher's Wink

'If they're demonstrating in bloody Honiton of all places,' Frisby said, 'we'd better prepare for the revolution. I took a holiday there once and everyone was tucked up in bed by six.'

'I'm still keen on the water cannon pic,' Harry said.

'But only because it's got a couple of dolly birds with most of their clothes blown off, you dirty sod. The political angle's not strong enough. A bunch of not very sexy exhibitionists...'

'And the prime minister's son.'

'Who's not in the shot. And who's a licensed clown. Of course give him a mention, but there've been far better riots tonight. That Cumbrian sheep stampede, for instance. Forty Labour activists hospitalised by blue-dyed herdwicks. The Farming Fraternity party speaks! And what about those hand-to-hand jousts on the Norfolk broads? Five yachts, two motor cruisers and a houseboat sunk, and fifty missing presumed dead after being tossed off a paddle steamer.'

There was a tap on the door and the picture editor bustled in with an armful of fresh prints.

'Above Cleethorpes!' he gasped, taking the top one off the pile. 'Look – huge inflatable boobs!'

'Your kind of thing, Harry,' Frisby said with the hint of a sneer. He was famously puritanical. 'What's it about, Bob?'

'Sky advertising by the Pink Party.' Half a dozen pink busts, securely tethered to the ground, floated a hundred feet in the air. 'But this second one's better.'

They saw a small single-seater plane, its occupant wearing first world war flying gear and leaning out to fire a pistol at the assertively nippled balloons.

'He's Fred Gormsthwaite of the Men Fight Back party. They're in line for half a dozen seats in the north.'

'The world's gone mad,' Frisby said sourly.

His phone rang, and he wandered off to talk. They heard him giving someone a bad time.

Wednesday

'Of course the man's a screwball,' he was saying, 'but he's *your* screwball, not mine. You put him in charge of the party, for God's sake. No, in charge of the *country*, which is far worse. We told you not to do it, remember. You thought our man was too extreme. Well!'

He came back towards them, twisting a finger around his temple to indicate that he was speaking to a half-wit.

'I'm not prepared to play any more games, Gerry,' he said. 'I held back on the footling Freddy story for you, and then you repaid me by letting his old man off the leash.'

He sat down heavily in his chair, suddenly looking very weary.

'All right, he snapped the leash himself. But so what? And listen, Gerry, I really don't need to hear any of your subtle off-the-record hints that he's been seeing a shrink. Worried friends say, etcetera. On one alarming occasion he even etcetera. Please not! Of course he's nutty. Anyone who quotes Karl Marx is, by definition, nutty in my book. I've simply lost interest!'

He pressed the red button and tossed the phone on to the desk.

'There's nothing for it,' he said in despair. 'We'll have to go with Muckle.'

*

When the kindly man called at his home, Taz thought for a nasty moment that he had come to ask for his computer back, but all he wanted to do was give him yet another little scoop.

'I've been so very impressed by your blog,' Fitzroy Julian purred, 'that I thought you deserved one last story before election day. You do have a most exceptional following.'

He had brought a typed script, as before. Old head and young head bent over it together.

'I know something about his son,' Taz said. 'He's no good, is he? A bit wild, yeah?'

'It's in the family. As you can see from reading this, his father isn't quite the ticket.'

'But he's the prime minister, sir.'

Julian laughed.

'I applaud your respectfulness, but very few of them have been what you'd call quite normal.'

'Like that Lady Thatcher in the picture, perhaps?' he asked innocently. There was no need to explain which picture he was referring to. 'I've heard it said . . .'

He tailed off, and this time Julian's laugh had a different timbre.

'Ah, we have to tread carefully there, Taz,' he warned. 'We're on holy ground, you see. Some regard it as blasphemy ever to utter . . . but come on, let's proceed.'

Taz began translating from the English language into his own.

> Some of yew bros hef called in doubt de cre-denshuls of de Tory party after tings wot dat strange cat Sturgeon (yep, dats in troof how dey bap-tised de poor brat) Warbytton bin sayin these past few daze.
>
> He may be deprime minister of our grate nashun, folks, but he bin soundin off like some commie in de kremlin in moscow town, wiv creepy talk of showerin benfits on de poor and dat kind of wild infatuation.

'How's this going, sir? Is that infatuation right?'

It was so wonderfully wrong that Julian knew that it was wonderfully right.

'Press on,' he encouraged him.

> So here's de terrible troot, frenz. Warbytton is off his pathetic head. Man, he's half way to de moon loony!

Wednesday

> Wot nobody but yew knows, cos its right dis moment ex-clusive to dis blog, is dat dis weirdo Warbytton saw the inside of a police cell dis evenin after crazy antix on de South Bank leadin to a riot. The fuzz detained him after he was seen prancin in oddball disguise wearin massive shades to hide his stinctive visage. Course, being the pre-mier, dey let him go without charge, but his frenz say its time he took a dive outa public life for de good of hisself and us all.

'Nearly there,' Julian said. 'This is splendid.'

'Are you sure you want me to add the last bit?' Taz asked. 'After all this grabby stuff about the crazy dude, it sounds a bit like the usual political crap. No offence meant, sir.'

'Oh, it's vital, Taz. I mean, it's what we call an *endpiece*. It gives the whole thing a rounded feel, believe me.'

'If you're sure.'

> So wot all dis means is dat the Conservative Party is free of all dis shit, frenz. Wot he's bin sayin is not dere policy, bruvs. De big man is one loco honcho, but yew can safely put your cross agin a Tory name and know its helpin to make the nashun strong and safe.

'Good man,' Julian breathed, reaching out to shake his hand. 'I'll see myself out.'

After he had gone, Taz sat immobile before the computer for some minutes. He felt calm and yet profoundly dissatisfied. He asked himself whether he had ever taken a decision in his life – about anything important at least. He had always been a dutiful son, even though it meant wasting hour upon tedious working hour in a warehouse full of carpets whose dust got up his nose. He had been a mild, insipid lover, lacking the inner fire – the balls, in short – to see off an exciting rival. And this acceptance of Felix Julian's demands: wasn't it passivity, weakness and capitulation all over again?

He returned to the screen and wrote a final paragraph.

> But dat's juss the party line, amigos. Yew show me one politico dat's not full of da brown stuff. It comin out of dere ears, folks. Dat's why I says agin, don't put your cross agin dere sorry names. In dis life yew hef to vote for yusself. Amen!

After pressing the button to send the blog on its way, he closed down the computer, reached for his phone and deftly thumbed a message.

'Chloe,' he texted, 'where are you?'

THURSDAY

The English were in shock. About themselves. It had always been a comforting myth that the Celtic fringes were excitable and unreliable, but it appeared, after all, to be the stolid John Bulls who had been driven practically unhinged by election fever.

Reports from the north suggested that the Scots had scarcely donned an extra tartan in nationalistic pride, while lugubrious Welsh nationals regarded Westminster goings-on with their customary surly indifference and the Irish tribes busied themselves with time-honoured quarrels of their own. Only England awoke on polling day to a whiff of smoke in the air from a thousand disturbances and to a fluttering of St George's flags up and down the land.

Election posters had been widely pulled down, trashed and defaced – sometimes, as was the way of it, by unmannerly political opponents, but just as often by affronted supporters who had found their dearest causes shockingly betrayed.

How the disaffected hordes switched their votes would doubtless keep psephologists occupied for months to come. In the meantime, it was Applied Mathematics' cantilevered legs that provided the morning's earliest guide to the state of the parties.

'A bit of a shift to Excalibur, Martin,' chirped Melissa the night nurse, bringing him his breakfast tea at half past five. It was such a convenient time for their shift pattern. She'd be off in half an hour, and her replacement had better things to do, what with paperwork and the rest of it, than to make an early appearance on the wards. 'Crept up by three since last time I looked.'

'Coont curr lez!' he grimaced through his dressings.

Drinking tea was impossible without help, but poor Melissa certainly didn't have time for that kind of luxury. It was non-stop from the moment she arrived, and Power4Us had all her timings monitored.

'Mind you, there've been quite a few ripe comments on your other peg,' she said.

A marker pen sat next to his water jug. One of the staff had made a list of the parties on the plaster encasing his right leg, and every passing nurse, doctor, surgeon, phlebotomist and anaesthetist, not to speak of every visitor to every other patient in the ward, was encouraged to indicate a preference, each painful time swinging his helpless limb about in the process. The cast on his left leg was, the inked heading read, for 'Observations'.

'You'll never believe what someone's called that Monty Muckle!'

'Coont . . .'

'How on earth did you guess that?' she asked.

*

Diana Warbytton had been dreaming of suffragettes. She led a plucky gang of them, all sporting pompoms, but when, with great daring, she threw herself in front of a horse at the races it lowered its head, opened its mouth and spouted a great gout of water at her. The flood kept coming and coming, tossing her this way and that, until she opened her eyes and found, with a mixture of relief and disappointment (she was, after all, in revolutionary earnest), that she was in the bed that dear Freddie had so generously given up for her.

So this was Downing Street, HQ of the oppressors – always excluding dear daddy, of course. He was now a hero, after their shared exploits of the night before. What a triumph it had been

Thursday

to be thrown, however briefly, and not really quite thrown if one wished to be tiresomely accurate about it, into a prison cell!

She slipped out of the bed and rifled through the drawers of a dressing table until she found a pair of nail scissors. Tugging the bedhead away from the wall, she sat on her haunches and scratched the word FREEDOM on the back of it. Then she returned under the covers, where she lay beatifically smiling.

Diana had joined the Pankhurst sisterhood.

*

'Bucks fizz,' Freddie said, bringing a tray to the bedside. 'And I'm the buck.'

Blonde curls stirred on the pillow.

'We're the fizz,' Serena giggled, squirming contentedly on the Egyptian cotton.

He handed her a flute and took another around the bed to deposit it on the table at the far side.

'Breakfast's up!' he called, climbing into the sheets with his own.

Raven-haired Popsy came padding in from the bathroom, looking a little less the archetypal librarian. Without her lost spectacles the world was a vague blur, and yet she unerringly found her flute and slid in next to him.

They all clinked rims.

'Drink up,' he said, 'and then it's on to our next course.'

'Such fun!' the two girls chimed together.

*

It was a tinkle on her phone that woke Chloe. She was in another strange bed, but this time a single one. The walls on her small room were smothered in artwork. There were, indeed, no etchings, but she recognised a carelessly splashed Pollock, two cruel Bacons, three migraine inducing Rileys and a veins-and-all Lucian Freud study of Stretton Mathers, stretched to the gaze with such blotched and crimped genitalia as to make her exceedingly grateful for her night's solitude.

It had been a wonderful evening. While Ben, the artist's slender, young, dapper Sri Lankan lover, had cooked a meal of a dozen spiced taster courses, Mathers had given her a tour of his walls and a hilariously, often brutally, frank account of his outrageous life and times.

'A stranger in paradise!' he called out now, tapping at her door.

'I certainly don't know anyone stranger, Stret,' she smiled as he came in with a tray.

'And you'll feel you're in paradise when you've drunk Ben's pick-me-up,' he promised, 'though God knows what exotic vegetation and wildlife he's incorporated. If it moves, spit it out.'

'I've just had an email,' she said.

'How terribly old-fashioned.'

'From someone called Larry Turnbull Jenkins at Central Saint Martins.'

'A lousy artist,' Mathers said. 'The three names is a give-away.'

'Leonardo da Vinci?'

'The da doesn't count.'

'Henri Toulouse-Lautrec.'

'Neither do hyphens.'

'John William Waterhouse.'

'I rest my case. But Larry's a good administrator if you like that sort of thing. What does he want?'

Thursday

'He's offering me an integrated masters course.'

She did look blissfully happy.

'Of course you won't want to get bogged down in all that soul-destroying academic baloney,' he said. 'Timetables, lectures, examinations. Gives me palpitations just to think of it. Shall I dictate a polite refusal?'

'Are you kidding?' she grinned.

He patted the bed where he supposed her knees to be.

'Just don't use your middle name,' he said.

*

PC Dunnock's first call-out of the day promised to be tiresome. The local discount store had apprehended, as he had been trained to say, a 'foreign gentleman' caught shoplifting.

'Two satsumas, a tin of sardines and a ball of string,' the store detective said, handing him a green passport. It had some strange lettering on the top and then Republic of Uzbekistan.

'Come on, mate,' the felon said, still in possession of the incriminating evidence. 'It ain't much. You can turn a blind eye this once, can't yer?'

There was something not quite right, Dunnock thought. More than one thing. He struggled to remember, if he had ever known, where Uzbekistan was and what kind of people lived there, but this rangey black fellow in a floral shirt, beach shorts and sandals reminded him of every Jamaican he had ever met. And although he had no idea how natives of the place usually spoke, it was surely amazing that this newcomer had so quickly adopted the capital's working class argot.

'Your name, sir?' he asked, with practised politeness.

'Isn't it in there?' He indicated the passport. 'I haven't got my reading glasses with me.'

Dunnock pondered long and hard. He wasn't too sure that the photograph matched, but it had suffered severe water damage. He read the name three times and gave up.

'Can't possibly pronounce that,' he said. 'But it says you're the trade minister of Uzbekistan.'

'Does it?' He peered inside. 'Well, of course I am.' His face brightened. 'Does that mean I can claim diplomatic immunity?'

'Perhaps it does.'

'Then I will. Count it as claimed. Thank you.'

He peeled one of the satsumas and began to eat it.

*

Ellie had never known Mr Gripp late before. Greg. She looked out of the window and beheld the queue of claimants with horror. The trick was to keep them waiting for twenty minutes before opening the door, although this fine spring weather sadly lacked the softening-up effect of winter frost and rain. How would she cope with the inhuman horde without her masterful boss to tame them?

He arrived just in time but was not his commanding self. One arm was doubled up in a sling, while the other cradled a stout crutch with which, adopting a curious swinging motion, he awkwardly manouevred himself towards her.

'Greg! My . . .'

She couldn't quite bring herself to utter the endearment, but how tragic it was to see such effortless authority brought low.

'That blasted Rosejoy!' he exclaimed.

'Curvature?'

'He was the ringleader, Ellie. The evil genius. I thought I saw Bell's Palsy and Double Hernia lurking in the shadows, too. I can't prove any of it or there'd be condign punishment, believe me.'

Thursday

'Condign, indeed,' she said, not knowing the word. 'What happened, Greg?'

'It was by the London Eye last night. Damn fine speech by the Labour chappie. Quite unexpected. He even used a phrase of mine – pain with justice. I hadn't meant to stay, but he had us so fired up that a group of us were raising our fists in the air and chanting. Pain with justice!'

'It must have been wonderfully stirring,' she said.

'And then these riff-raff got to work, and it was too much for the police to handle. When I caught Rosejoy's malevolent eye I knew there was trouble coming.'

'You did say he was an athlete.'

'Not that he did the dirty work himself. Signalled to some of his able-bodied mates – even more able-bodied, I mean – and they came for me with wooden staves and iron bars. As you can imagine, Ellie,' (he felt himself deliciously carried away), 'I gave as good as I got. Hurled three of them over the wall into the Thames.'

'Oh, Greg!'

He shuffled back to his chair and fell into it.

'God,' he said, watching the handout claimants struggling into the waiting room, 'I'm going to give these bastards such hell today!'

*

For Jessica Warbytton the halcyon days were nearly over. She loved her dear old Eggie, but much better at a distance. Later today he would be home to attend the count, and after that, if Veronica's finger had gauged the pulse as sensitively as usual, she would be seeing a lot more of him.

'Even if the party scrapes home,' she explained, 'there's not the slightest chance they'll keep him on as prime minister.'

Lady Thatcher's Wink

'Why on earth not? He's such a fine figure of a man.'

'But there's a bit more to it than that, mummy. Policy, for instance.'

'Policy! Not at Eggerton Manor, please.'

'Some of them do care about that kind of thing, you know, down there at Westminster. And I'm afraid daddy hasn't exactly been playing the game.'

'Oh?'

'I won't worry your head about the sordid details. But it's not inevitable, you know, that he'll even be returned as our MP. Have you seen all those St George flags along the high street?'

'Very patriotic.'

'They're for the Excalibur party.'

'The *what*?'

'Oh, do go and feed the horses, mummy!'

And so that's what Jessica did – that and take the dogs for a hike over the fields, thin the gooseberries and arrange to spin into the village later to take cake and tea with her oldest chum, Claudia. She was enjoying her free time while she still had it.

*

Ben Strutters, summoned to the chief constable's office, stood stiffly to attention, until a wave of the hand suggested that he could relax a little. But he wasn't invited to sit down.

'I've heard reports of what happened on the South Bank last night,' the chief said, 'but I want to hear it from your own mouth, inspector.'

'Sir.'

'The violence appears to have been extreme.'

'There were several groups of armed trouble-makers, sir.'

'I'm talking about *our* violence.'

'Ah, yes.'

Thursday

'Water cannon?'

'We did down a good many ruffians with the deluge gun. A few legs broken, I have to admit. Some blood.'

'Anything else?'

'Staves next, sir.'

'Indiscriminately?'

'Depends what you mean, sir. Anyone who had the look in their eye, if you know what I mean. No questions asked.'

'And then the Tasers?'

'As a last resort.'

'But then you went in heavily with them.'

'That's true, sir. Twenty people felled on the spot, four of them hospitalised.'

'And what do you say, inspector, to a criticism in today's *Blither*' (he gathered the newspaper from his desk and squinted at it) 'that your use of force was disproportionate in that eighty members of the public were injured while one police officer sustained a bruised thumb and six of his colleagues lost their helmets?'

'I'd say, sir, that the public learned a useful lesson.'

The chief constable reached out a hand.

'Exactly the right response, inspector,' he said. 'I'm fast-tracking you to superintendent.'

*

Lambert Probus had thought he might enjoy a day as acting prime minister now that Warbytton was on his way home, but he should have guessed that there might be a crisis cunningly awaiting its moment.

'How can I help?' Felix Julian asked, breezing happily into his office, tail wagging at the suggestion of conflict.

'A sticky incident,' Probus said. 'You remember that press

Lady Thatcher's Wink

attaché with the Uzbek trade delegation? The one we thought must be secret service.'

'Has to be. Speaks perfect English. That's the clue.'

'He rang me from Heathrow to complain that his minister wasn't being allowed out of the country. The delegation was due to fly out an hour ago and the plane's still on the tarmac. I'm afraid I was a bit short with him.'

'Short?'

'Well, I told him that we don't tolerate corruption in this country, however illustrious the individual. A trade minister caught filching satsumas, canned fish and a ball of string from a supermarket has to expect due process of UK law, especially at a time when we're inflicting ever grosser punishments on our own people for low-life demeanours.'

'He's a common thief, Bertie?'

Probus seemed about to cry.

'I think there's been a horrible mistake, Flix. The police arrested someone with the minister's passport earlier this morning, and they weren't bright enough to realise it was the wrong man. Now that ghastly attaché is threatening us with all sorts of consequences, and in impeccable English – there was even a Shakespearian reference. He mentioned the United Nations.'

Julian smiled.

'Leave it to me,' he said at his oily best. 'What's the deal we made with them? Warplanes?'

'Half a dozen.'

'We'll throw in one more for luck. That always works.'

*

Warbytton sat back in his first class carriage, accompanied only by a flat parcel of brown paper and roughly tied string, and felt gloriously at peace with the known world. What had been a narrow belt of terrain had stretched its boundaries somewhat thanks to those heady voyages of exploration with his adorable Chloe, but he hadn't the slightest wish to travel any further. Why seek some other newfoundland? Hadn't he always been amiably content with contentedness?

The countryside sped by with a similar amiableness: spring lambs, sprouting cornfields, the first leaves breaking tawny gold on the oaks. He would never, ever step into Downing Street again and, although he enjoyed well enough the simple duties of a rural MP, he would be a happy man if he was never again obliged to enter the gloomy palace of Westminster.

He closed his eyes and thought of his green acres; of his favourite corner with its leather armchair and crystal tantalus; of Jessie in one of her milder moods. With the rich, homely smell of their fur seeming to rise in his nostrils, he particularly looked forward to worming the spaniels.

*

Gerry Turtle had never imagined that he would hear himself say it, but his directions to the taxi driver were given without ironic overtones or the slightest theatrical raising of the eyebrows: 'To McDonald's restaurant in the Edgware Road.'

'I know who you are,' John Carrot said as soon as they had spun round and were wedged in a queue of traffic. 'You're that Tory spin doctor we always see on the box.'

'Possibly.'

'Oh, definitely mate,' Carrot said, as if confirmation were needed. 'Always putting the world to rights, aren't you?'

He was a combative man by nature, but ever since his beloved Arsenal had been relegated from the premiership the previous Saturday (and dumped four-nil by their great rivals,

Lady Thatcher's Wink

Spurs, to make it even worse) he had been at war with the world.

'I met your prime minister once,' he went on. 'He seemed to think stags were a road hazard in London. Is he nutty?'

'Completely,' Turtle said. 'He's taken to quoting from the Communist Manifesto. Who will you be voting for?'

'Don't know that I'll bother. They're all the same.'

As they drew up outside the eatery he saw Gloria alighting from another cab. They kissed flatly three times and crossed the threshhold.

'You'd better order,' Turtle said. 'This is new to me.'

'You think it's my bistro of choice?'

'But it's anonymous,' they said together, just as they had once been verbally locked at the *Ham & High*.

Seated with their burgers and coffees, they said nothing for a few minutes on end. All hope seemed to have drained out of them.

'What have we done?' Gloria said at last.

'It's too late to ask.'

'What on earth happened to Warbytton? That's what started it all.'

'I wish I knew. We've tried to stitch him up as a crazed loner, but he's far from frothing at the mouth. It actually seems to be some kind of weird socialist conversion.'

'He actually believes in helping the poor?'

'And the sick, for Christ's sake.'

'Imagine a society run like that. A world for wimps.'

'It's hard to credit, but perhaps it's a reaction against my coaching. Perhaps I trained him too hard.'

'But you have to whip them into line, don't you? Mine's an absolute mule.'

They both forgot that they had already paid, and sat waiting for the bill to come.

Thursday

'Is your polling as bad as mine?' Gloria asked. 'It's looking like a melt-down.'

'A disaster. Inevitably. They don't like change, do they, the great British public? Frightened out of their conventional little wits by anything but the slightest tweak to the status quo. You and I had it all nicely arranged for a neck-and-neck contest, and then that Warbytton clown decided to turn everything on its head.'

'Leaving the field to . . .'

Nothing more needed to be said. When they parted outside the restaurant their clinch was much closer than before, cheek to cheek in ancient amity.

*

'Good afternoon, Mrs Threadgold,' Daphne said, meeting her outside the polling station. 'Have you placed your vote?'

'Yes I have, dear. And I'm sure you're not trying to winkle out of me which way I've gone.'

'I wouldn't think of it.'

'Because it's a secret ballot, and that's one of the glories of this great country of ours, I'm sure you'll agree. It's part of our hallowed tradition . . . *Hallowed*.'

She had never used the word before and quite liked the sound of it.

'And hard won, Mrs Threadgold,' Daphne said doggedly. 'In our case by a bitter fight against what they call the forces of reaction.'

'I'm not sure about that. I'm not very keen on bitterness. Live and let live, I say.'

'I mean votes for women. They didn't want us to have that, did they?'

'Depends who you mean by *they*, doesn't it?'

Lady Thatcher's Wink

'Men mostly, I've always thought. But then again, the men at the top never wanted to give it to those at the bottom, did they? Always a bit of a struggle, wasn't it?'

'I'm sure our dear monarchy has always wanted what's best for the ordinary people they rule over.' She sniffed. 'Not that I'm saying it's anything to do with the way I just voted.'

'Of course not, Mrs Threadgold. See you in the usual place tomorrow, and don't forget your vouchers.'

*

'We need to talk,' Taz said to his father.

'Is this carpets, Emre?'

'It's man to man, father.'

'Oh dear. It's sexual matters supposedly. I need to prepare myself.'

'No, father. It's about work. About my career.'

'You don't have a career, Emre. You have a share in this warehouse when I pop off. Isn't that all?'

'I mean that I need to stand alone, to have a life outside rugs and carpets.'

'But what could that be? This is some strangeness afflicting you perhaps.'

'I wish to give my notice, father.'

'Your notice? As if this were some office employment and you my clerk?'

'Something like that.'

'And what notice do you give? A week, perhaps? Or a month? So that I know.'

'A year, father.'

'You give notice of a year? I never heard of such an interim in these matters. You can't do that thing. And, in any case, where will you go?'

Thursday

'That's why I need a year. To sort myself out.'

'In that case, Emre, sort yourself out and *then* give me your notice.'

'All right, father. I hereby give you notice that I shall give you notice in a year.'

*

'What's an equerry?' Monty Muckle challenged, giving Dalton Frisby a cocky thumbs-up. He had a phone to his ear and his feet on the desk, revealing a pair of St George cross socks. 'Is that so! Sounds a pretty cushy life to me, my friend. And how do I know you *are* one?'

The Excalibur leader was having the time of his life. Nobody yet knew whether he was about to be carried shoulder high by a jubilant mob into Downing Street, as his imagination liked to stage the event: what mattered was that people thought he just might.

'And what's his majesty's view on that?'

People like the editor of the sodding *Daily Maul*, who had spent so much ink on rubbishing him for months past. Now the slimy toad was desperately trying to make up for lost time, sucking up to him while still putting on his hard-nosed journo act. Muckle enjoyed that sort of game.

'Tell his maj there's no prob. I'll sort it. Back to sharpening the quills, pal!'

He returned his feet to the floor.

'A policy debate?' Frisby asked hopefully.

'Wouldn't you like to know, Dalton!' Muckle guffawed. It was a stupid name, but as he'd been invited to use it he would give it the full orotund works. He put a finger against the side of his nose. 'Trade secrets, Dalton.'

Frisby had called in his top team to meet the potential man

Lady Thatcher's Wink

of the hour. They knew how serious he was when they saw the open drinks cupboard and the bottle of scotch on his desk. None of them dared approach it before yard-arm time and a distinct invitation, but Muckle was already helping himself to a second glass.

'We were wondering, weren't we Harry,' Frisby said, 'how this House of Lords reshaping will work.'

'Frankly, is it constitutional?' his news editor asked bluntly.

There was silence, apart from a faint clinking of ice.

'Oh, was that question directed to me, mate?' Muckle said eventually. 'I'm the last person to ask. That's a detail I'll happily – in the event, natch – leave to the man who knows best.'

'Your attorney general?' wondered Arnold Snitch.

'His sovereign majesty, of course. Come on, that's what the people want! Don't you people know that?'

'It's always been our duty to speak for Middle England, Mr Muckle,' Frisby said quietly. He felt piety descend upon him. 'Everyone turns to the *Maul* to know what to think and how to behave.'

'Ho, ho!' Muckle chortled. He rocked the scotch in his glass. 'And what can your great organ do for me?'

It took him a couple of seconds to hear what he had said.

'*Great organ!*' he exploded, his eyes dancing.

Then his phone rang again, and the feet returned to the desk.

'Freeman Goodblow,' he intoned. 'That rings a bell, as the duchess said to the bishop.' He gave Frisby another thumbs-up. 'Yes, of course I remember. How could anyone forget?'

Their discomfiture was pleasurably palpable. They sat in silence, spare parts at a wedding, dying for a drink.

'I'm delighted to embrace all believers in the cause, old chum,' he said. 'Though perhaps I should watch the embrace where you're concerned, ha! ha!'

Thursday

He kept the conversation idling along. He had all the time in the world.

'Yes, we'll talk if it happens, Freeman. But tell me a bit more about that sex den . . . Was it really? . . . How often? . . . Oh, I'd love to have been there!'

He eventually rang off and reclaimed the whisky bottle.

'The former prime minister,' he said needlessly.

'With an offer?' Frisby tried.

'A scoop for you, Dalton,' Muckle whispered confidentially. 'Are you ready for it?'

The news editor grabbed a pad and pen.

'It was all a lie about them cats,' Muckle said.

*

Dear Lord Macklethorp,
After giving many years of my adult life to the service of the Daily Excess, I must, with the deepest regret, tender my resignation.

In short, sir, I find that I can no longer reliably safeguard and mount the step-ladder with which the company has thoughtfully provided me, in part because standards of public life have so far diminished that there is no longer proper respect for the person, particularly if he is of a marginally challenged physique, or for such valued appurtenances as the said object.

My resignation, my lord, depends, as you will realise, on my receiving due recompense for my long labours on your behalf. On receipt of your kind assurances I shall be happy to send you, in a plain envelope and to whichever address you may care to designate, the interesting photograph that we once very briefly discussed.

Yours truly,
Bernard 'Titch' Tupper

cc Wright Malarkey, solicitors

*

'Pigeon shit,' Youssef said. 'That was our rub in the bad old days, mister. No lie! This cream smell a bit tastier, yes?'

Alan Sprout almost gurgled with pleasure. He was feeling so abnormally, so ridiculously relaxed that he idly wondered, without the slightest accompanying worry, whether he'd suffered a stroke.

'Of course you very naughty man,' Youssef raised a hand to wag a finger. 'Too much sunning. Too much scratching. You ruin it all in no time quick, yes? Now we have to clear up.'

His old life had gone. He had fled in terror from the South Bank the previous evening knowing that it was all over. No sensible electorate would vote him into power, and thank God for that. Why had he ever let himself be talked into it? Into any of it? He was going to resign from every political allegiance as soon as all the ballyhoo was over. He was going to give more time to his allotment. He was going to renew his subscription to the model railway magazine. He was going to romance Edna all over again.

'I give you three pots to take away with instructions how to use,' Youssef said. 'You keep on rubbing and everything goes pretty damn quick, yes?'

'A labour of love,' Sprout smiled.

'And you sure I not give you a little dragon for luck?'

He breathed deeply. The desecration of his chest had been torture, but would a little pricking on his upper arm be so very dreadful?

'A heart and arrow here, Youssef,' he found himself saying. 'With an A on one side and an E on the other.'

*

Valmai Partridge was sipping a latte at a pavement cafe when she saw her adversary approaching.

Thursday

'Gormsthwaite!' she yelled. 'Come here, you creep!'

He limped closer. He might be the epitome of a flying ace when airborne, but she thought him a pretty poor specimen on the ground.

'You attacked my boobies!'

'Men fight back,' he grinned.

'But they cost me all of two grand,' she told him, 'and they were only exposed up there for an hour.'

'How much do you think it cost me to hire that plane?' he countered. 'Not to speak of the ammo. Anyway, this is war, Valmai.'

'To the death, Fred. Won't you join me for a coffee?'

*

From Sir Hilary Miles-Trumpington, Trustees Office, Royal Academy of Arts

Dear Chloe (if I may),
I have been asked to enquire whether you might consider exhibiting your drawings and paintings at the Academy in the autumn. We have been greatly impressed by the quality of your work recently publicised in the national media, and would regard it as a COUP//*TS1 ALERT!* to be allowed to curate it. You will know of our international reputation, and I can assure you that your portfolio would be mounted to the very best advantage and under your own supervision.
With respectful thanks,
H M-T

*

'Don't tell me,' Felix Julian sighed, summoned by Probus to yet another crisis meeting in the Thatcher room. 'The passport office has managed another of its cock-ups.'

'Same story, new twist. The Uzbeks are all on board with their paperwork, but the plane can't move.'

'I don't deal with technical issues.'

He was met with an unaccustomed glare.

'Who put the Russians in charge of the flight tower, Flix?'

'Ah! It's a trial run for when they take over. Don't they know how to wave the flags, or whatever it is they have to do?'

'It's political. It seems the Russians and the Uzbeks aren't very good friends at the moment. Something to do with gas supplies.'

'It was gold and copper before that. They never need much excuse to squabble, if the truth be told. The Foreign Office has told both sides to grow up, but for some reason they don't seem to listen to us.'

'That's all very well, Flix, but how do I force this obdurate Ruskie to take the scowl off his face and let them go?'

'That's difficult, isn't it? After all, it's their business, not ours. It may be a matter of persuasion rather than force.'

Something was nagging at the back of the Probus mind.

'You're not trying to tell me that Heathrow isn't part of the UK any more.'

'The land is ours,' Julian said, 'right down to the earth's core.'

He went to the door and called loudly for the faithful Jonathan, who soon stepped inside, wiping his steel-framed glasses with a handkerchief.

'Sorry to bother you,' Julian said with a disarming smile, 'but the chancellor has forgotten the details of the air traffic control agreement. I think you were involved in drawing up that legislation.'

'It was a typical state sell-off,' Jonathan said. 'A ten-year contract with the usual sweeteners.'

'Those being?' Julian probed innocently.

Thursday

'Total lack of interference mainly. Is there a problem?'

'Oh, shit!' Probus said.

Julian gave a sardonic bow.

'May I go now?' he asked.

'No you bloody well can't,' Probus said. 'I haven't told you about our second problem. Lord Botting.'

'Of Botting. Something to do with arms sales?'

'To do with art. Botting lent us that Thatcher portrait, and now he wants it back for all the dirty stuff to be cleaned off.'

'And?'

They all turned their eyes to the wall.

'It's gone.'

There was, indeed, an empty space.

'The lady vanishes,' Jonathan said without missing a beat. 'I'd call this an opportunistic theft, sir. It was definitely there last night.'

'What are we going to tell Botting?'

'Blame the Uzbeks,' Julian said drily.

*

Was it his imagination, or did the union flag above the palace really stir in the breeze more jauntily than ever before?

'Once and future,' he murmured.

'What's that, sweetie?' his queen consort asked idly, lifting her pen from the newspaper. She rarely heard anything the first time he said it. 'Would you happen to know any large rivers in South America?'

'The Amazon.'

'No, that's not right.'

'I've been there, for God's sake! Damn fine opera house in the jungle. Fell asleep during Aida and had to persuade them I'd been counting the beats.'

Lady Thatcher's Wink

'It's seven letters and the fourth one's N.'

'Not the way I'd ever think of spelling it.'

He lowered his gaze towards the Mall, where scattered drifts of his people dawdled and mingled in the bright May sunlight. His people and a heavy overlay of tourists, it had to be granted, yet undeniably *his*. The constitution said so, the court flummery corroborated it (how he adored the obsequious kneeling of ministers at privy council meetings) and the national anthem gloriously hymned it, but on this auspicious day it was impossible not to consider, not to keenly await, a fuller kind of possession.

'One can't but think of that earlier Charles,' he admitted.

'Shouldn't think too hard,' she laughed. 'Not when you know what happened to *him*!'

'I rather meant the second one,' he said. 'The merry one. The restoration, and all that.'

'And Nell Gwynne with her oranges, but don't build your hopes up on that score. Are there two r's in interregnum?'

'It's probably optional. The English language is a free-for-all these days. Choose your own grammar! And every ruddy newspaper spells king without a capital letter.' It was another of his hobby horses. Perhaps, if everything went well, he would have a new law passed to stop all that nonsense in its tracks. 'But should I trust that Muckle fellow?'

She gave him a guarded smile.

'He's so . . . different, isn't he?' she said.

'Not one of us.'

'I should rather hope not. People of that . . . breeding . . . are just so unpredictable, aren't they?'

He paced the floor, hands clasped behind his back. (It put her in mind of a trussed turkey.) For too many cruelly frustrated years he had, with a few notorious lapses, constrained his urge to publicly put the world to rights. Now that it was so close to

Thursday

becoming *his* world, one which actively encouraged him to throw his royal weight about, the fear that the triumph might be snatched away from him was almost too terrible to bear.

'I've been promised the Lords,' he said, 'but it doesn't have to stop there, does it?' (He was muttering and gesticulating, she thought, like a Shakespearian actor performing a soliloquy. This audience wasn't exactly spellbound.) 'Not if the people like what I'm doing, surely? I could, given time, extend my powers...'

She seemed to look through him.

'Posturing fool,' she said.

Arms still waving, lips still moving, he left the room and began to climb the stairs to his private apartments.

'Seven letters,' she added, not realising that he had gone. 'Begins with B.'

He stood before the full-length mirror in his dressing room and composed a face. Then he rang a bell on the wall and, while he waited, tried another.

'Your majesty?' asked Pimpkin, appearing in the doorway.

'This expression.' He beckoned him forward. 'What does it tell you?'

He puckered his lips in a tight smile and inclined his head to one side.

'You have the beginnings of a migraine, sir?'

'Blast it no, Pimpkin! This time...'

The lips parted a little, and the eyebrows were raised.

'Perhaps, sir, that you have a little secret you're unwilling to divulge.'

'Oh, God!' Sometimes he wanted to seize his secretary by the throat. 'What I'm after is simply condescension without a trace of arrogance and above all tempered by a sort of saintly kindliness. Is that too much to ask?'

'Not in the least, sir.'

Lady Thatcher's Wink

'Tell me, Pimpkin. What do the common people make of me?'

'That you're a remarkable monarch, sir.'

'It's honesty I want, Pimpkin.'

'That you're a very remarkable monarch, sir.'

Even now those sturdy commoners were queueing outside polling stations north, south, east and west, many of them, just possibly most of them, anxious to throw aside the long, wan centuries of parliamentary servitude and, with touching gratitude, bend the knee once again before a leader known to be above the sordid political fray of left and right.

He waved a dismissive hand at Pimpkin and, once alone, rehearsed in front of the mirror.

'I am almost tearfully proud,' he began, a sinewed hand adjusting the imagined crown on his balding pate, an imagined crowd swarming beneath his balcony, 'to stand here as both your master and your servant.'

Was that mastery business a tad *de trop*? No, anything less would be a betrayal of the millions crying out to be swept up in the royal embrace, to be cured of their existential misery by a touch of the monarch's healing hand.

'Ever since that other great Charles returned to claim his crown in 1660, we and our subject people have forged a bond which is the envy of the world.'

Yes, he heard the roar. He felt the adulation. He sensed (who was it had said that?) the hand of history upon his shoulder.

'I commend those worthy members of parliament who have sweated so strenuously on your behalf, and I recognise that they still, for an interim period, have a role to play in our national life. Let them fulfil their humble duties in the Commons while my appointees in the Lords busy themselves with the essential matters of state.

Thursday

'In due course, I have no doubt, you, the mighty British people, will make further demands of the Crown that I and my descendants shall be happy to obey, until this great nation is once again the fully-fledged monarchy that so many of you wish it to be.

'We are, my people, together waking from a democratic nightmare – and now, perchance, to dream . . .

"*Lady Thatcher's Wink* takes the excesses and injustices of politics in Britain today and magnifies them – but is it for satirical effect or a warning of what might be around the corner?

David Arscott paints a colourful collection of characters, most of them unappealing, a few saved from this only by their own naivety. You will chuckle at the absurdity of it all, but this is a dark humour, set in a world as depressing as anything from Orwell, and worryingly one that may seem increasingly less far-fetched as time goes on."

– **Norman Baker**, *former Liberal Democrat MP and minister in the 2010–2015 coalition government.*